P9-DOH-908

Stagecoach Pursuit . . .

As Longarm stuck his head out the window, he saw all four cutthroats moving up to within ten feet of the coach. He managed to dispatch the one-eyed hombre, send him rolling off his horse's hip before getting his boot caught in a stirrup. The horse dragged him, screaming, off the trail and across the rocky desert.

Longarm raised his rifle again. The closest rider, wearing a blue calico bandanna, raised his own pistol, narrowing an eye to aim down its barrel at Longarm. As the lawman triggered the Winchester, he saw his opposing shooter's pistol smoke, heard the roar, and felt the hot slug cut an icy furrow across his left cheek.

At the same time, his own slug punched dust from the rider's pinto vest and threw him back against his cantle. The cutthroat triggered another shot skyward as he screamed, dropped the pistol, and rolled down his blaze-faced dun's left hip. He, too, got a boot caught in a stirrup, and as the horse careened off the trail and into the rocks and prickly pear, the rider went bouncing along beside it, his bandanna ripping off in the wind, his screams dwindling quickly beneath the din of the stage and the hammering hooves

DON'T MISS THESE
ALL-ACTION WESTERN SERIES
FROM THE BERKLEY PUBLISHING GROUP

THE GUNSMITH by J. R. Roberts

Clint Adams was a legend among lawmen, outlaws, and ladies. They called him . . . the Gunsmith.

LONGARM by Tabor Evans

The popular long-running series about Deputy U.S. Marshal Custis Long—his life, his loves, his fight for justice.

SLOCUM by Jake Logan

Today's longest-running action Western. John Slocum rides a deadly trail of hot blood and cold steel.

BUSHWHACKERS by B. J. Lanagan

An action-packed series by the creators of Longarm! The rousing adventures of the most brutal gang of cutthroats ever assembled—Quantrill's Raiders.

DIAMONDBACK by Guy Brewer

Dex Yancey is Diamondback, a Southern gentleman turned con man when his brother cheats him out of the family fortune. Ladies love him. Gamblers hate him. But nobody pulls one over on Dex . . .

WILDGUN by Jack Hanson

The blazing adventures of mountain man Will Barlow— from the creators of Longarm!

TEXAS TRACKER by Tom Calhoun

J.T. Law: the most relentless—and dangerous—manhunter in all Texas. Where sheriffs and posses fail, he's the best man to bring in the most vicious outlaws—for a price.

TABOR EVANS

LONGARM

AND THE
SANTIAGO PISTOLEERS

J

JOVE BOOKS, NEW YORK

THE BERKLEY PUBLISHING GROUP
Published by the Penguin Group
Penguin Group (USA) Inc.
375 Hudson Street, New York, New York 10014, USA
Penguin Group (Canada), 90 Eglinton Avenue East, Suite 700, Toronto, Ontario M4P 2Y3, Canada
(a division of Pearson Penguin Canada Inc.)
Penguin Books Ltd., 80 Strand, London WC2R 0RL, England
Penguin Group Ireland, 25 St. Stephen's Green, Dublin 2, Ireland (a division of Penguin Books Ltd.)
Penguin Group (Australia), 250 Camberwell Road, Camberwell, Victoria 3124, Australia
(a division of Pearson Australia Group Pty. Ltd.)
Penguin Books India Pvt. Ltd., 11 Community Centre, Panchsheel Park, New Delhi—110 017, India
Penguin Group (NZ), 67 Apollo Drive, Rosedale, North Shore 0632, New Zealand
(a division of Pearson New Zealand Ltd.)
Penguin Books (South Africa) (Pty.) Ltd., 24 Sturdee Avenue, Rosebank, Johannesburg 2196,
South Africa

Penguin Books Ltd., Registered Offices: 80 Strand, London WC2R 0RL, England

This is a work of fiction. Names, characters, places, and incidents either are the product of the author's imagination or are used fictitiously, and any resemblance to actual persons, living or dead, business establishments, events, or locales is entirely coincidental.

LONGARM AND THE SANTIAGO PISTOLEERS

A Jove Book / published by arrangement with the author

PRINTING HISTORY
Jove edition / August 2010

Copyright © 2010 by Penguin Group (USA) Inc.
Cover illustration by Miro Sinovcic.

All rights reserved
No part of this book may be reproduced, scanned, or distributed in any printed or electronic form without permission. Please do not participate in or encourage piracy of copyrighted materials in violation of the author's rights. Purchase only authorized editions.
For information, address: The Berkley Publishing Group,
a division of Penguin Group (USA) Inc.,
375 Hudson Street, New York, New York 10014.

ISBN: 978-0-515-14827-5

JOVE®
Jove Books are published by The Berkley Publishing Group,
a division of Penguin Group (USA) Inc.,
375 Hudson Street, New York, New York 10014.
JOVE® is a registered trademark of Penguin Group (USA) Inc.
The "J" design is a trademark of Penguin Group (USA) Inc.

PRINTED IN THE UNITED STATES OF AMERICA

1 2 3 4 5 6 7 8 9 10

If you purchased this book without a cover, you should be aware that this book is stolen property. It was reported as "unsold and destroyed" to the publisher, and neither the author nor the publisher has received any payment for this "stripped book."

Chapter 1

She was one of those rarefied Mexican beauties with sparkling, coffee brown eyes, a low-slung, cleavage-heavy bodice, and long legs that, even concealed by a gold-embroidered red traveling skirt, seemed to be yearning for something to straddle.

Sitting across from this beauty in the pitching, jostling stagecoach that was doing wondrous things to that bodice and the ample contents within, Deputy United States Marshal Custis P. Long, known to friend and foe as Longarm, was having the devil's own time keeping his eyes off of her. There just wasn't much else to look at. In trying to keep his eyes from boring unattractive holes in the girl facing him, he slid his gaze to her right only to see the bloated, craggy, gray-bearded face of a dozing Butterball hardware drummer in a shabby green-checked suit.

The lawman gave a frustrated chuff and raked his gaze, albeit slowly and appreciatively, across the girl's radiantly beautiful, delicately chiseled face—with a fleeting and involuntary glance at the bodice that seemed to be inviting an out-and-out, eye-bulging stare—to the man riding to her left.

Longarm had gathered that, impossibly, this was the woman's husband, and he couldn't have looked more like a Southern dandy if he'd been supporting himself in his seat with an ivory-handled walking stick, sporting a planter's hat, and having a butler brush the dust from his coat while serving him cognac in crystal a goblet.

The dandy wore a tailored brown suit that, in spite of the liberal coating of trail dust, had obviously cost more than Longarm raked in for his lawdogging services in three hard months. A *norteamericano*, he had a baby-soft face with prim, light green eyes, sandy hair cropped close beneath his brown beaver hat, and a handlebar mustache with waxed, upturned, and twisted ends. His lips were constantly pursed and his eyes bored into Longarm as though daring the federal lawman to let his eyes stray to his wife once more.

So Longarm looked up at the ceiling and then said to himself, *Ah, the hell with it*, and let his gaze fall upon the girl for a leisurely though not totally indecorous appreciation.

To his surprise, he found her eyes on him. She dropped them demurely, and her regal cheeks flushed slightly. She fiddled with the crucifix in her slender, almond-colored hands, and gave a delicate cough. Returning her gaze to Longarm, she said in a heavy Spanish accent, "Would you mind pulling the shade beside you, señor? The dust is irritating my lungs."

Longarm's eyes dropped of their own accord, as though to investigate the organs in question, only to have his loins nipped once more, hotly, when he saw the two jostling, light tan mounds pushed up and secured by the lace-edged bodice. Their size was accented by the small, jade-set silver crucifix hovering just above her cleavage.

"Of course, señorita." Longarm pulled the deer hide shade over the window to his right.

"That's *señora*," said the dandy in a prim growl with a petal-soft Southern accent. "The lady is bound by holy matrimony."

Longarm glanced between the girl and the dandy and pinched the brim of his snuff brown hat at the Southerner. "Congratulations. You've made a most enviable conquest."

The dandy's eyes flashed wickedly at Longarm's bold remark. The girl's cheeks turned a darker shade of red, and she looked down while nervously recrossing her legs beneath her skirt, inadvertently brushing her calf against one of Longarm's. At least, he assumed it was inadvertent. When she let her smoky gaze flick across the cramped aisle, holding Longarm's eyes for a heart-wrenching second, the lawman grew doubtful about how inadvertent the touch had been, and the stifling air in the stage bounding through southern Arizona's sun-baked chaparral grew hotter by several degrees.

To cover his discomfort, not to mention the rare blush he felt rising in his sun-leathered cheeks, Longarm leaned toward the dandy, extending his hand. "Name's Logan Lang, heading for Santiago. Who might you folks be?"

He gave the phony name because he was on his way to pick up a prisoner from the sheriff in Santiago, Arizona. There were none too few men in the local environs—namely from the ranch the prisoner's prosperous, powerful father owned—who didn't want to see the young firebrand, an accused killer named Wesley Wade, trucked off to Denver for trial and, likely, an appointment with the hangman. Longarm had been warned by his boss, Chief Marshal Billy Vail of the First District Court, that he might be stopped either en route to Santiago, or while on his way back to Denver with the young ringtail, Wade, in tow.

Thus not only his phony handle but also his cowboy attire, consisting of plain wool shirt, brown leather brush jacket, red neckerchief, and black denim trousers stuffed into his traditional cavalry boots, well worn by years and many miles. Longarm knew the boots were a little out of sync with the rest of his puncher attire, but he valued healthy feet. Often, he had to run as well as ride, and nothing mangled a man's dogs worse than pointy-toed boots built for toeing stirrups and little else.

Those incredible breasts and rich, wanton lips across from him, the lawman thought, could soothe even the worst case of twisted heals. But his reverie was interrupted by the woman's husband, who leaned forward with a haughty chuff to squeeze Longarm's proffered hand, and the lawman suppressed such lewd musings to give his best disarming smile.

"Name's Malcolm Mayfair," the dandy purred. His well-bred plantation manners did not let him exclude his wife from his introductions. "And this," he added, canting his head to the girl, "is my wife, Raquella Mayfair." He gave both "wife" and "Mayfair" a little extra emphasis. He obviously not only resented Longarm's attentions to the exquisite beauty beside him but had little time for shit-stomping cow nurses.

"Pleased to make your acquaintances, Mr. Mayfair," Longarm said, leaning back in his seat and pinching the brim of his snuff brown hat—which was the second item of his traditional attire with which he refused to part—at the girl and saying, "Ma'am. Or, señora." He chuckled, plainly addled by the lustrous brown eyes and swollen lips before him. "Both handles seem so doggone formal."

"Would 'Raquella' make you more comfortable?" the girl asked.

"She would at that." Longarm chuckled again and slid his eyes at the dandy scowling at him from beneath trimmed, sandy brows. "I mean, uh . . . the name 'Raquella' would be a little easier on the tongue—yes, ma'am."

"And what do you do for a living, Señor Lang?" asked the girl, her lustrous brown eyes red-tinted by the sunlight angling around the sides of the drawn window shade.

"I'm what some would call a drover, Raquella. I deal in cows . . . when I can get a job, that is."

"You're out of work?"

"At the moment."

Longarm felt awkward, drawing out the lie like this. Raquella Mayfair was the type of young woman—he doubted she was over twenty—you wanted to tell your whole life story to. The real one. And then you wanted to sit back and, drowning in those eyes and anticipating closing your mouth over those lips that likely tasted of just-ripe cherries, hear her own life's tale as well.

"But I'll no doubt run into something soon, maybe closer to fall roundup time."

The girl's husband said in a tautly admonishing tone, "And how is it you find yourself out of work, Mr. Lang? There seem to be plenty of ranches around. Surely one must be hiring."

Longarm had to think fast. It wasn't easy with those beautiful tits jostling in their tight nest only a few feet away. "Just a run of hard luck, you might say, Mr. May-fair. A little disagreement with the ramrod can go a long way in gettin' you run off a place on a hot, greased track."

"Ah," the dandy said, dropping his chin like a school-master upon finding the culprit who'd planted the bull-frog in the girls' privy. "A bit of a brawler, are we?"

Longarm hiked a shoulder and feigned chagrin. "I reckon you might say that."

"You're a very big man," noted the girl, more color rising in her cheeks as her eyes drifted across Longarm's chest. "And broad in the shoulders . . . with powerful arms and hands. You must be a wicked one in a fight. Like my brother, Ubre." The girl paused for a half second, eyes narrowing slightly with remembering. "He could never ride into our village from my father's rancho without getting into a fight. A big man, Ubre. Almost as big as you, Señor Lang. But it is not good to fight. My brother came to a bad end because of fighting, and I warn you—you may, too."

Longarm's heart warmed at the genuine concern in the girl's eyes. He was about to tell her not to worry about him and then to ask about her brother—an emi-nently curious creature, this beautiful girl—but before he could open his mouth, the driver yelled down from the boot, "Salt Creek Station acomin' up! Fifteen minute breather, folks!"

The girl, dismissing her conversation with Longarm, leaned over her husband to pull the shade away from the window, peering out and squinting her almond-shaped eyes against the dust. "We are somewhere finally. My legs get so cramped." She straightened and waved a hand to indicate the heat. "So thirsty!"

"I offered you water just a bit ago, pet," the dandy reminded her in his customarily condescending tone.

"Yes, but it is warm. I want a cool glass of water, Malcolm."

"Out here, you must drink what you can get or die of dehydration." Mayfair glanced at Longarm. "Isn't that right, Mr. Lang?"

Before Longarm could respond, Raquella set her jaw and retorted, "If I was indeed dying, I would drink your water, Malcolm. But since I am not dying, I would prefer cold water that does not taste like the brandy from your wretched flask."

The drummer sitting to the right of the girl, having awakened from his doze to get in on the tail end of the conversation, chuckled at the girl's pluck. The dandy chastised him with a frown, and the drummer sniffed and snorted, cowed, and opened the shade on his side of the stage to look out the window at the corrals and barn pushing up along the trail.

When the stage had rocked to a halt, the dust growing thicker as it caught up to the carriage, Longarm lifted the shade on his side and peered out at the low-slung, adobe-brick shack before which the stage had stopped. Six horses were tied to the hitchrack fronting the place, and from his perch he could make out a Chain Link brand blazed into the hindquarter of a star-backed dun that had turned its head to inspect the newcomers. The horse's bit had been slipped from its mouth so it could draw water from the stock tank in front of it.

Longarm remembered from his pre-trip conference with Billy Vale that the ranch his prisoner's father owned was the Chain Link. As warning bells tolled in the lawman's head, he half-consciously raked his left hand across the walnut grips of his double-action Frontier Model Colt .44-40, to make sure the weapon hadn't left the cross-draw holster high on his left hip. Longarm had given the well-aged scabbard a fresh rubdown with hog tallow before he'd left on his current mission, and he'd carefully taken apart the Colt and cleaned and oiled it. He'd done the same to his Winchester '73, which leaned against his left thigh, and again with the double-barreled, over and under, pearl-gripped derringer riding hideout in his right jacket pocket, connected by a gold-washed chain to the old dented and tarnished railroad watch residing in the left pocket.

Seeing the Chain Link horses, he was glad he'd taken the time with his accoutrements. Arizona Territory boasted nearly as many border toughs as riled Apache Indians, and then there were the ranch hands who'd likely been ordered to see that the deputy U.S. marshal coming for a certain rancher's son was filled with hot lead and turned toe down in a deep ravine.

Chapter 2

Longarm grabbed his rifle and stepped off the stage, holding the door wide for the others. The driver, Eli Fischer, came ambling back from the driver's boot, swiping his shabby hat at his dusty denims, wheezing from the pleurisy he'd picked up over the winter and shaking his head. He peered at the station house as he muttered just loudly enough for Longarm and the other passengers to hear, "Might be best if the señorita remain aboard the stage."

"Why is that?" Raquella Mayfair had already gained her feet and was standing crouched in the doorway, sticking her pretty, black-haired head out, dark brown eyes sparkling in the sunlight.

Longarm followed the driver's gaze to the station house's brush-covered front gallery and saw nearly a half dozen reasons why the man was right. Sitting in wicker chairs or perched on the rickety looking railing were five men and one woman. The men, judging by their shabby trail garb in stark contrast to their impeccably cared for and numerous weapons—were obviously border toughs.

One of the men—a hatchet-faced half-breed with a big bowie knife in a shoulder scabbard—had the girl, a young Mexican, sitting on his lap. She wore only a short, flour-sack skirt. Her feet were bare, and so were her breasts. The half-breed's head was bent low to the girl's chest. He had his hands up under her skirt, clamped against her little rump, as he nibbled and suckled her bare, brown bosoms.

The girl chuckled and pulled at the half-breed's ears, glancing shyly over a fragile shoulder to peer back at the dusty stage. She wasn't the only one looking at the carriage. The eyes of the other four men were riveted on Mrs. Mayfair. One of the men—all of whom were Chain Link riders, Longarm figured—was so taken by the Mexican girl leaning out of the stage that a lit cigar fell from his lips to bounce, sparking, off a chap-covered thigh to the floor. If he was aware of it, he ignored it.

A man sitting with one hip on the railing and who wore a patch over one eye with a vicious, jagged scar beneath it groaned from deep in his chest. It was a low wail of animal craving.

It appeared the Chain Link riders hadn't seen a woman of Raquella Mayfair's caliber in a month of Sundays.

"Yes," said her husband, peering out the stage door from behind her. "It might be a good idea if you waited in the stage, pet."

Raquella's face hardened defiantly. "I need to stretch my legs. And I want a glass of water." She extended her left hand to Longarm, who helped her out of the stage and into the dusty yard. Looking up at him, she said, "You'll escort me inside, won't you, Mr. Lang?"

"That'll be enough of that, Raquella," her husband growled, stepping down from the stage and regarding the men on the gallery with a wary gaze. "If anyone is going to escort you, that man will be your husband."

The jehu, Eli Fischer, tugged at his beard as he, too, appraised the hard cases still staring at the girl with animal lust—even the half-breed who'd been nibbling the Mexican *puta*'s breasts. "I don't recommend anyone escort her anywhere but back inside the coach. Yessirs, I do believe that's just where this young lady oughta remain till we can get the teams switched."

"Nonsense," Raquella said. "I'm tired and thirsty."

She took her husband's arm and smiled up at him. "A cold cup of water please, Malcolm."

The dandy muttered an oath under his breath and said through a strained smile directed at the gallery, "Of course, pet . . ."

Longarm stepped back and watched the two climb the gallery steps. He held his hand taut around the neck of the Winchester resting on his right shoulder but couldn't help admiring the feline sway of Raquella's round rump inside the tight-fitting traveling basque.

Apparently, the men on the gallery were admiring it, too—that and much more. As Raquella and her husband crossed the gallery to the station house's open front door, the half-breed cursed awfully in Spanish and stood up suddenly, throwing the half-naked *puta* to the floor, where she landed with an indignant yelp and cried, *"Bastardo!"*

Longarm glanced at the driver, who knew Longarm's true identity, as the lawman had patronized this stage line before, but Fischer had vowed to keep his secret. "I reckon I'll go on in and keep an eye on things," Longarm said.

Fischer gave his beard another couple of hard pulls as
he looked over the men and the angrily sobbing whore.
"You do that, Mr. Lang."

As the driver turned to help the shotgun messenger
and the hostlers who'd come up from the barn with fresh
horses, Longarm took a deep breath, hooked a thumb in
a pocket of his black denims, and casually mounted the
gallery steps. Apprehension gnawed at him. The Chain
Link riders were probably keeping an eye out for a man
wearing a badge. In fact, they probably paid a visit to the
relay station here at Salt Creek every time a stage was
due, sniffing around for the federal who'd been sent for
their boss's son.

Still, one of them might recognize Longarm even in
his cow waddie duds. As long as the deputy U.S. marshal had been fighting crime throughout the West, he'd
made quite a few more than his share of acquaintances.
But your average cowhand west of the Mississippi was
little smarter than the cows he nursed. So it wasn't sur-
prising that they let Longarm stroll across the gallery
and into the shadowy interior of the station house without so much as a raised eyebrow.

It helped, of course, that they were all having wet
daydreams about the lovely Mexican creature who had
just passed before them . . .

With more luck like the kind he was having here,
Longarm might be able to nab Wesley Wade from the jail
in Santiago, put him on a horse, and get him all the way
back to Denver with the Chain Link boys being none the
wiser until they read in the local paper about the necktie
party held in Wesley's honor compliments of the U.S.
Federal Government.

Longarm stopped just inside the open door, surveyed

the broad, dark, low-ceilinged room that was fetid with the sour smell of spilled beer and tequila. Flies buzzed unseen in the darkness. From the ceiling emanated the squawks of bedsprings and the guttural groans of love-making on the second floor.

Fifteen feet beyond Longarm, Raquella and her husband were taking chairs at a round table on the far side of a square-hewn ceiling joist from which a dusty ristra hung. Malcolm was scrubbing the table with a bright white handkerchief and shaking his head, casting occasional looks of disgust toward the ceiling, above which a girl was groaning and a man was calling her dirty names in English.

A bar ran along the room's right side. The other two stage passengers, the hardware drummer and a sallow-faced cowboy in a spruce green duster, stood facing the bar, each with a shot glass in his hand, both glancing cautiously out the dusty window off the end of the bar at the gallery where the hard cases milled.

Behind the bar stood a wizened, stoop-shouldered oldster with long, stringy gray hair and a thick mustache and goat beard of the same color. His blue eyes were washed out and expressionless, but they were riveted on the dandy and Mrs. Mayfair, his hands crossed almost respectfully behind his back.

Longarm didn't recognize the gent. The stage lines out here usually had a high turnover in help, and at the moment that fact made Longarm's job much easier. He always felt foolish sidling up to acquaintances he ran into while undercover and asking them to keep mum about his profession. It made him feel like a freckle-faced boy playing make-believe in his own backyard.

Yeah, his luck was holding. He just hoped the Mayfairs' did, too . . .

Longarm walked over and laid his rifle on the counter. The old gent seemed to have some trouble tearing his gaze from Raquella Mayfair, so Longarm helped him with: "You don't have any Maryland rye, do you, friend?"

The oldster frowned as he turned to Longarm. "What kinda rye?"

Longarm shook his head dismissively. "Just rye. Any kind." He tossed some coins on the bar, where they rolled around while the old gent, glancing over his shoulder at the Mayfairs, grabbed a bottle from the shelf behind him.

The old gent had just set the bottle and a shot glass on the counter when Malcolm Mayfair, sitting at the table beside his wife, the dandy's beringed hands entwined on the wooden surface before him, said, "Barkeep, we'd like a glass of cold water and a brandy. And, if you wouldn't mind"—he lifted his head to stare through the two dusty windows onto the porch where the Chain Link boys were kicking around, speaking in low tones—"hustle it on over. The lady and I are in a bit of a hurry."

The old-timer glanced at Longarm. Longarm hiked a shoulder and grabbed the rye bottle. While he splashed whiskey into his glass, the old-timer dippered water from a bucket behind the bar, filled a shot glass from a brandy bottle, and hustled it creakily out from behind the bar and over to the Mayfairs' table.

"Gracias, señor," Raquella said graciously, lowering her tin cup from her rich, damp upper lip.

Malcolm plucked a coin from his vest pocket and deposited it in the barkeep's hand as though it were the key to El Dorado. The barkeep looked at it.

"Uh . . ." he said. "The brandy's ten cents more."

"Good Lord," Malcolm said with a weary air, and fished another coin from his vest pocket. "Better be damn good brandy."

As the barkeep ambled back to the bar, looking at the coins in his palm suspiciously, Malcolm sipped his drink. Longarm didn't watch to see how the man reacted to the hooch, because the drummer said beside him just loudly enough for Longarm to hear, "What in tarnation is a girl like that doin' with a nancy boy like *him?*"

He hooked a clandestine purple-nailed thumb to indicate the two behind him.

Longarm was as befuddled as the drummer, but the undercover lawman only hiked a shoulder, propped his elbows on the bar, and lifted his rye to his lips for a gingerly swallow. It may have been rye, but it had a good dose of gunpowder in it as well. And probably a few other things that made it about as rotgut a grade of tarantula juice as Longarm had ever tasted. It cut the trail dust, however, and buffed the edge off what had been a long, dusty stage ride from Las Cruces.

It should be over soon. One half of it, anyway. If Longarm's recollection was right, they were only about thirty miles from Santiago, the little border town nestled at the base of the Apache Bluffs, within a day's ride of Nogales farther to the southwest.

Pretty country. He wished he was going fishing or elk hunting there, with a two-week-long vacation stretching out ahead of him. Him and his pal Cynthia Larimer—the buxom, indigo-haired favorite niece of Denver's found-

ing father, General William H. Larimer—going camping
by a spring-fed stream and riding bareback, double and
buck naked, diddling to make the hawks and coyotes
blush.

His reverie was interrupted by the thump of boots and
jingle of spurs. He looked into the fly-stained back bar
mirror to see the five Chain Link riders stroll into the
station house, the long-haired half-breed first, thumbs
hooked in the pockets of faded denims. A slender, hide-
wrapped braid hung down the side of his head, and one
wandering eye gave him an added menacing look. The
two pistols and two big knives he was armed with didn't
do anything to temper the impression of a wanton killing
machine.

Flanked by the one-eyed hombre, he strolled straight
back past the Mayfairs' table, the other three men tramping single file behind him and his partner, two smoking
quirleys, one absently spinning a Schofield revolver on
his right index finger, dropping it into its oiled holster
and pulling it out again quickly. He did this absently, as
though he were merely practicing his fast draw in the
privacy of his own room.

Raquella and Malcolm sat in their chairs like statues,
moving only their eyes to follow the five hard cases to
the table directly behind them.

"Ah, hell . . ." breathed the drummer beside Longarm
and pressed his bulging potbelly taut against the bar, sort
of tightening his arms against his sides defensively.

Longarm remained leaning over his elbows, drink in
his left hand, leaving his right hand free and within striking distance of the Winchester '73 lying across the bar
beside him. He watched the hard cases drag chairs out
from the table behind the Mayfairs' and, sighing and

grumbling, one man chuckling lewdly, sag down into their seats. The half-breed straddled his chair backward, about four feet behind Raquella and Malcolm. He crossed his arms over the chair back, rubbed his nose on a hairy forearm, and sniffed.

Neither Malcolm nor Raquella looked at him. They both kept their heads facing the open door from which emanated the smell of hot horses, the clanking of harness buckles and chains, and the stomps of shod hooves.

Longarm sipped his rye, keeping his eyes glued to the fly-specked bar mirror and on the hard cases flanking the half-breed. They lounged back in their chairs or leaned forward on the table, smoking and leering and snorting. The sounds of lovemaking from the second floor had fallen silent, replaced by the dim murmur of a man and woman's clipped conversation.

Longarm slid his eyes across the hard cases, trying to get a fix on each one's cold-steel expertise. He'd already judged the one with the Schofield a tinhorn, and the one he'd worry about least if it came to a lead swap. He didn't want it to come to a lead swap, because innocent people got hurt in lead swaps. Like as not, Malcolm was no hand with a six-shooter. In fact, Longarm hadn't seen a gun on the man, unless he was carrying a hideout.

But when it came to close-quarter hoedowns and the chips were stacked against him, Longarm always thought it favorable to know who to hoe down first.

Longarm wished Eli Fischer would call everyone back to the stage. He didn't have the authority to do it himself, but he was about to do it anyway when the half-breed ran his nose across his dirty forearm once more, then reached inside his shabby leather jacket and pulled out a rawhide pouch. He hefted the pouch in his hand, then tossed it through the air between Malcolm and Raquella, who gasped and jerked sideways as though she thought the pouch was a knife.

Her exclamation was punctuated by the *thud* and *chink* of the coins hitting the table.

"Twenty dollars," the half-breed said in labored guttural English, poking a finger at the ceiling. "For one half hour. Upstairs. With the señorita." He grabbed his crotch and grunted goatishly. "My loins ache for her!"

The one-eyed man snickered, showing toothless gums.

Chapter 3

Longarm had to admit that his own loins ached for the señorita. But then, she'd make any man's loins heat up like a smithy's forge. He doubted that a mere half hour with such a creature would even begin to do her justice, and the twenty dollars offered by the half-breed was downright insulting.

He didn't wait for the dandy, who sat frozen in his chair, his face bleached the same white as his starched collar, to turn the offer down. For one thing, he wasn't sure the poor, frightened man wasn't considering it, and for another, he was tired of the half-breed's bad manners.

In the station house's pin-drop silence, he threw back the last of his rye, slammed his shot glass on the counter, picked up his rifle, loudly racked a shell into the chamber, and swung around to face the five grinning, snickering cutthroats. The half-breed turned toward him, and the man's black eyes widened in shock as Longarm drew a bead on the man's broad chest.

"Fuck!" the man screamed, snaking a hand across

his flat belly toward the big Colt residing in a shoulder holster.

He hadn't gotten his hand wrapped around the pistol's bone-handled grips before Longarm's Winchester roared, blowing off about six inches of the half-breed's left rear chair leg and pitching him back into the table behind him with an indignant yelp. Longarm ejected the spent brass, which *ping*ed off the bar top and rolled to the floor, then racked a fresh round before drilling off the right rear leg of the half-breed's chair, pitching him in that direction so that he resembled a drunk sailor on choppy seas.

"What?" the half-breed screamed, twisting around to cling to the table behind him. *"You tryin' to get yourself killed, amigo? You don't like life?"*

Two more blasts of Longarm's Winchester, and the half-breed was sitting only about a foot above the floor, his legs spread wide. He was supporting himself with his hands on the floor. He regarded Longarm with a combination of bald-assed fear and tooth-gnashing fury.

But he said nothing, only stared at Longarm, mesmerized, utterly baffled.

The other hard cases had sat frozen in their own chairs, staring with much the same expressions as the half-breed. The one-eyed man's arm moved, his hand no doubt sliding toward a sidearm beneath the table.

Longarm's Winchester roared once more, drilling a ragged hole in the middle of the hard cases' table with a loud *whunk!* The one-eyed man jerked back, raising both arms to his shoulders. One of the other men winced and grunted, twisting a little in his chair; apparently, the slug had nipped some leather off his boot.

Silence.

Longarm stared down the smoking barrel of his Winchester, his brown eyes hard.

The Mayfairs leaned low over their table, both regarding Longarm with fear and beseeching.

Boots thumped on the porch. Eli Fischer poked his bearded head into the room, looking around warily. He held an old Trapdoor Springfield carbine up high across his chest. The shotgun messenger, a young string bean with red hair and cow-stupid eyes and holding a double-barreled shotgun as though he had no idea what to do with it, stood behind the driver, his lower jaw hanging.

"Well," the jehu said, fingering his matted beard, "I see how we was all just startin' to have fun, but I reckon it's time to hop aboard the stage for the next leg of our journey. Don't dally, folks. I got a timetable to keep!"

He glanced at Longarm, then stepped back away from the door, gesturing for the shotgun lad to do the same. Longarm looked down his Winchester barrel at the five Chain Link riders, who remained frozen to their chairs— even the half-breed, though his chair was considerably lower than the others and he was having to balance on his hands and boot heels.

"You heard the man," Longarm said, sliding a commanding glance at the Mayfairs, then at the sallow-faced cowboy and the Butterball hardware drummer at the bar. "Get a move on."

The hard case who'd been pretending he was Billy the Kid with his Schofield started to rise from his chair.

"Not you, Billy," Longarm growled at him as Raquella and Malcolm quickly raked their chairs back and, glancing cautiously over their shoulders at the hard cases, made their way to the door.

Longarm didn't need to tell the cowboy and the drummer twice, either. They were across the room and out the door on the heels of Malcolm Mayfair in seconds.

As the passengers were climbing aboard the stage, the jehu looked through the station house door once more. "You comin' there, uh, Mr. Lang?"

Longarm wished the man could use his phony handle a little more naturally, but at least he'd used it instead of complicating the situation more by alerting these men to his true identity.

"I'm right behind you, Mr. Fischer," Longarm said, keeping his Winchester trained on the hard cases. "I'm findin' it kinda hard to say goodbye to these nice fellas."

"All righty, then."

Fischer stomped down off the porch. Longarm sidled toward the door, hearing the stage's thoroughbraces squawk as the potbellied jehu and the string bean shotgunner climbed into the driver's box.

"You boys sit tight, have another drink," Longarm growled. "I see any of your faces again . . . and I mean *ever* . . . I won't be near as patient as I been here this afternoon."

"This wasn't none of your affair, amigo," the halfbreed snarled, his jaws drawn so taut his cheeks were dimpling.

"Now you tell me."

Longarm backed through the door and stopped, making sure none of the cutthroats moved. If they were typical of the other men Norvell Wade had riding for him, Longarm didn't want to trifle with the rest.

"We'll meet again, friend," piped up Billy the Kid with wooden bravado, cutting his eyes around at his friends.

"Your funeral, Billy."

The stage had started forward. Now Longarm turned, lowered his Winchester, and dropped down into the yard.

Quickly, he untied all five of the Chain Link horses from the hitchrack, then pumped two quick rounds into the air over their heads. When the horses had galloped off, buck-kicking and whinnying, in all directions across the yard, Longarm jogged up alongside the bouncing coach and, sort of hop-skipping and planting one boot on the single wooden step, opened the door.

With one more backward glance at the station house, the porch of which was still empty, he ducked into the stage, grabbed a ceiling strap, and turned to close the door behind him.

When he'd retaken his seat across from Malcolm Mayfair, who looked as though he'd suddenly come down with the flu, Raquella looked at him with her glossy brown, relieved eyes. "*Gracias*, amigo."

"Don't mention it." Longarm held his Winchester barrel out the window as he plucked fresh cartridges from his shell belt and thumbed them into the rifle's loading gate. "But if I may be so forward, a girl who looks like you, Mrs. Mayfair, really oughta pick and choose her watering holes with more care."

Longarm kept an eye out for the Chain Link men, but all he could see of their back trail were rocks, greasewood, and barrel cactus, and the trail itself snaking through the broad valley between bald, craggy ridges rising to a brassy sky. The trail followed a dry wash sheathed in mesquites and occasional paloverdes, with here and there beyond it an old, weather-beaten log shack and a dilapidated corral hunkered along the base of a tawny-grassed knoll.

This was starkly beautiful country north of the San Pedro, but it was damned hard on those who tried to settle it.

Longarm decided that if the Chain Link riders were determined to come after them, they'd likely be so long running down their scattered horses that the stage would be pulling into Santiago before they caught up to it. And once in town, Longarm could rely on his play being backed by his old friend and San Isabel County sheriff, "Buckshot" Pete Peckinpah.

Having fought outlaws for the past twenty-five years, Buckshot was known as the best lawman in the territory— in fact, one of the very best lawmen the frontier had seen since the War Between the States. Buckshot Pete had once taken down seven cutthroats riding roughshod over a town that the mossy-horned badge toter had all but tamed on Colorado's Western Slope, armed with one pistol and the sawed-off 10-gauge shotgun from which his "Buckshot" moniker had been born.

Buckshot Pete had grown up in northwest Texas where, when he hadn't been fighting border toughs and Mexican horse thieves, he was running down marauding Comanches or the Comancheros who'd supplied the Indians with guns. Now, with most of the towns in Colorado Territory all but tamed—aside from a few mining camps here and there—Buckshot had settled down in the last town and county he'd put on a leash, Santiago, where Longarm had been told he was holed up with his daughter.

When the daughter had come or who the mother had been, Longarm didn't know. He hadn't seen his old friend in years and had only heard of the daughter second- or thirdhand from a mutual friend passing through Denver a few months back. Despite Buckshot Pete having a daughter to raise, Longarm was sure his old friend still had the bark on. Men like Buckshot Pete never lost it. And if the four hard cases did decide to further their argument and make another play for Raquella Mayfair, they'd rue the day they stomped with their tails up in Buckshot Pete Peckinpah's town.

Having taken one more satisfying gander at their back trail—as well as one more automatic peek at Raquella's low-cut bodice, in which her lovely breasts milled like dozing pups—Longarm tipped his hat down over his eyes and nodded off.

He'd just entered a dream in which, apparently bypassing foreplay, he was toiling lustily between Raquella's spread legs, when something woke him. He sat up, wincing at the wooden hard-on tightening his pants, and poked his hat brim off his forehead with his thumb. Raquella herself was just waking from a snooze and blinking her eyes, disoriented. Malcolm Mayfair had canted his head toward his window, peering out behind them.

"Oh, lordy," said the sallow-faced cowboy sitting to Longarm's left, dropping a newspaper to the floor and turning to look out the window on his side of the coach.

"What is it?"

Longarm had no sooner gotten the words out than another whoop sounded beneath the hammering of the iron-shod wheels and the thunder of the galloping team.

Raquella gasped.

Her gasp was punctuated by the spang of a bullet off a rock.

Raquella gasped again. "Heaven help us—it's *them*!"

Chapter 4

Malcolm pulled his head back into the coach. His flu bout had returned, his face bleached, eyes sharp with fear. "It's them, all right—God blast it, anyway!"

Longarm poked his head out his own window, squinting in the dust lifting from the wheels. Galloping riders were entering the trail from his side of the coach, about fifty yards back. Longarm couldn't get a good look at them because of the brush and dust and occasional boulders, but the loudening whooping and hollering and pistol shots made it plain who it was.

"Ah, hell!" intoned Eli Fischer from the driver's boot, echoing Longarm's sentiments exactly. "The bastards must have gathered their horses right quick and taken that dogleg trail through Juniper Bend!"

Longarm winced as another bullet screeched off a rock about ten yards off the trail, blowing up dust. He turned his head to yell toward the driver's boot, "How far to Santiago?"

"About seven miles!" Again, the jehu echoed Longarm's musings. "We ain't gonna outrun 'em, Custis. I mean . . . Mr. Lang!"

Longarm pulled his head inside the coach, and grabbed his rifle. The cowboy had his pistol out, but he held it like he wasn't sure what it was for.

"You know how to shoot?" Longarm asked him.

"Me?" The cowboy looked at the old, rusty Remington in his right fist. "I can shoot rattlesnakes and coyotes, if they're close enough. Me, I never tangled with no desperadoes before. Hell, I been working way up high in the rocks where there's no one much around but me and about thirty slow elk!"

"Keep it holstered, then," Longarm told him. "Don't want you shootin' one of us."

"Yeah," the drummer said, holding the two ceiling straps dangling ahead and to either side of him, sweating. "Don't want you shootin' none of us!"

Raquella looked beseechingly at Longarm. "Please, Señor Lang—don't let those savages take me!"

"Don't worry, pet," Malcolm said, rallying his nerve as he plucked a silver-plated, pearl-gripped .36-caliber Smith & Wesson from an ankle sheath. He opened the loading gate and closed one eye to inspect the wheel. "I'm no gunslinger, but I can protect my property."

"Just shoot what you're aiming at," Longarm said, poking his rifle out the window. He glanced behind at Malcolm, who was poking his Smithy out the window on the same side of the coach as Longarm. "And the back of my head ain't what you're aimin' at!"

Longarm could see the riders gaining on the coach, ducking their heads and squinting against the billowing tan dust. All five were there, three in front, then the one-eyed cutthroat, with Billy the Kid slightly behind him and wincing against the dust. The half-breed was the middle front rider. As Longarm clutched his rifle, racking a shell into the chamber, the half-breed extended a big Colt over his horse's head, grimacing.

The Colt puffed smoke and stabbed flames.

The bullet tore into the carriage housing just above Longarm's head. At the same time, the pistol's pop reached Longarm's ears—little louder than a branch snapping. He returned the shot, but the jostling stage made accurate shooting nearly impossible, and neither the half-breed nor the other riders so much as flinched as Longarm's slug sailed errant.

The lawman levered another round into the Winchester's breech, took aim again, and fired. This time the hard case on the left jerked his head to one side and lowered the pistol he'd been about to fire.

Longarm shouted up to the boot, "Quit jackrabbiting, goddamnit, Fischer!"

"Hang on, Custis—I'm sending Lonnie to help!" the jehu yelled back, then cursed as the half-breed triggered another round, which apparently came close to drilling the old driver.

Longarm raised his rifle and squeezed off two quick rounds. He'd aimed both shots at the half-breed, who seemed the most determined of the four hard cases, but it was Billy the Kid who took the bullet. The kid screamed, slapped a hand to his temple, and went rolling ass over teakettle off the rear of his galloping black-and-white pinto. He plopped into the dust and disappeared behind a bend in the trail, and the riderless horse, screaming, reins dangling, veered off into the brush and out of sight.

The half-breed glanced back, then turned forward again, grinning savagely and whipping his steel dust with his rein ends, urging more speed. He and the other three riders, hunkered low and kicking their mounts wildly, closed the gap on the lunging Concord coach as it slowed slightly for an upgrade.

Longarm pulled his head inside as the coach lurched and the carriage fishtailed between two steep sandstone walls. He heard a pistol pop to his left and turned to see Malcolm Mayfair triggering his snazzy popper out the opposite door's window, both the cowboy and the hardware drummer leaning far back in their seats as though to avoid a coiled rattler.

Behind the carriage, the cutthroats' pistols popped wildly. One bullet crashed through the coach's back wall and into the wall opposite, between the drummer and Mrs. Mayfair. The drummer cursed sharply. Raquella crossed herself, squeezed her eyes closed, bowed her head, and entwined her hands in her lap.

As Longarm stuck his head out the window again, he saw all four remaining cutthroats moving up to within ten feet of the coach. He managed to dispatch the one-eyed hombre, send him rolling off his horse's hip before getting his boot caught in a stirrup. The horse dragged him, screaming, off the trail and across the rocky desert.

As Longarm raised his rifle again, the leftmost rider, wearing a blue calico bandanna, raised his own pistol, narrowing an eye to aim down its barrel at Longarm. As the lawman triggered the Winchester, he saw his opposing shooter's pistol smoke, heard the roar, and felt the hot slug cut an icy furrow across his left cheek.

At the same time, his own slug punched dust from the rider's pinto vest and threw him back against his cantle. The cutthroat triggered another shot skyward as he screamed, dropped the pistol, and rolled down his blaze-faced dun's left hip. He, too, got a boot caught in a stirrup, and as the horse careened off the trail and into the rocks and prickly pear, the rider went bouncing along beside it, his bandanna ripping off in the wind, his screams dwindling quickly beneath the din of the stage and the hammering hooves.

Another bullet barked into the carriage housing near Longarm, flinging slivers at his face. He raised his rifle once more, then jerked with a start as an enormous, thunderous boom rose from above him. It sounded like thunder clapping a foot above his head.

At the same time, the rider galloping to the right of the half-breed looked as though an enormous tomato had smashed against his chest and belly. His arms flew straight up as though in holy euphoria. His hat blew off, and the two pistols he'd been gripping hit the ground. Dead instantly, eyes and mouth wide, he sagged back against his horse's ass, flopping wildly before careening off into the rocks and brush beside the trail.

Eli Fischer guffawed wildly. "You got him, Lonnie. Nice shootin', sprout!"

Longarm tried to draw another bead on the half-breed, but just before he'd started to squeeze the Winchester's trigger, the coach slammed over a chuckhole. The stage pistoned straight up and down before the right wheels left the ground for several seconds and then the left wheels did likewise.

"Mierda!" Raquella wailed.

"Shit!" screamed the drummer.

"Good Lord!" cried Mayfair, who'd pitched forward against Longarm.

"I think I'm gonna be sick!" screeched the saddle tramp, who was trying to disentangle himself from the drummer.

Just behind the coach, the half-breed bellowed something Longarm couldn't hear above the hammering wheels and the team's thudding hooves. Poking his head back out the window as he dropped his empty rifle and grabbed his revolver, Longarm saw the half-breed lift both his pistols toward the top of the stage. The guns roared, stabbing smoke and flames.

"Die, gringo!" the half-breed shouted, showing his tobacco-stained teeth in a devilish grin.

From the driver's boot, Fischer bellowed, "Oh . . . *mercy!*"

Again, Longarm was lining up his sights on the half-breed.

He glimpsed a shadow over his head, and looked up just as the shotgunner rolled off the coach's roof.

Longarm ducked and lowered his gun arm, but still the dead shotgun messenger knocked his hat off his head and tore his Colt from his hand as the body plunged straight down the side of the coach. The young man's head struck the shod wheel with a gut-wrenching *thud.* His long body spun before it hit the ground and rolled back away from the coach to disappear in the brush along the rocky trail.

The half-breed's pistol's popped again.

Fischer screamed.

The coach lurched sharply.

Longarm's balls rose into his throat as the rear of the carriage slid off the trail. The lawman turned his head forward just in time to see Eli Fischer's bulky frame pitch headfirst from the driver's boot. Fischer hit the ground with a clipped grunt and rolled like a rag doll into the rocks and shrubs along the trail, blood spraying from the twin wounds in the center of the dead man's back.

As the coach continued down the edge of the trail on only its right two wheels while the horses turned sharply left, Longarm drew his head back into the carriage. His brown eyes were large and glassy as he locked gazes with Raquella, who was clinging desperately to two hand straps. Her bosom jostled and shook, nearly springing free of its tight confines, while the men bounced and bobbed around her and Longarm like popcorn in a hot skillet.

"Hold on!"

As the stage pitched even farther onto its right side, its right two wheels no longer so much rolling forward as plowing up rocks and gravel and tearing sage shrubs, the Mexican beauty dropped her lower jaw in a terrifying realization of what was about to happen.

Longarm grabbed two handholds swaying free above his head.

They did him little good as the coach rolled completely over onto its right side and he was flung onto his back against the door, with all four other passengers tumbling on top of him.

The one grace note in the barrage of human flesh falling against him and punching the air from his lungs was that the first one on top of him was Raquella of the lovely, pillowy breasts, which, even in the chaos of the rolling stage and the rocks and dust being tossed by the shovelfuls through the windows and doors, Longarm couldn't help admiring. He even found himself enjoying the soothing albeit fleeting feel of them poking against his chest just before the stage rolled onto its roof and all the human occupants and whatever bags they had lying around violently switched positions.

Time seemed to slow down, and over the course of what seemed the next hour, Longarm found himself on top of Raquella and then sandwiched between the drummer and Mayfair, then, after another roll or two, between the drummer and the saddle tramp. All the while, the violently convulsing stage was filled with sand and grit and sage branches as well as the echoing screams of Raquella and the groans, snarls, oaths, and painful cries of the men.

Suddenly, Longarm was slammed onto his back so hard that fireworks blossomed behind his eyes. He convulsed like a landed fish, trying to rake air into his battered lungs. He was having trouble getting the air beyond a threadlike substance filling his mouth. It was like choking on a giant spider. Gagging and coughing, he opened his eyes.

Raquella was sprawled on top of him, belly down, groaning and squirming and moving her head around. Her hair was tangled like a big black tumbleweed. The lawman dragged a thick lock of her dusty hair from his mouth and managed to get a breath down into his lungs and back out again. His steeply rising chest roused the girl, and she lifted her head, her dark, befuddled eyes meeting his.

Longarm felt the twin warm bulges against his chest and looked down. Her breasts had all but sprung free of her bodice. The jade crucifix was wedged tightly sideways in her cleavage. He could see the entire pink nipple of one breast and the aureole of another. She was staring into his eyes, frowning as though deeply puzzled, wincing against the pain of the tumult, obviously addled.

When her vision seemed to clear a bit, she followed Longarm's gaze, saw her breasts flattened out against his chest, and whipped an angry, choleric look at him. She brought her right hand back behind her shoulder, and let it fly.

Crack!

His ears rang at the sudden blow. But he wasn't ungrateful. The blow seemed to clear his vision and cause the dusty stage to cease spinning around him. He also liked the exasperated set of Raquella's jaw and the straight line of her rich, full lips, the way her eyes seemed to cross as she squinted at him haughtily.

Someone groaned in Longarm's left ear. He turned to see Mayfair's head resting against Longarm's shoulder. The Southern dandy blinked his eyes and lifted his head, turned to Raquella, then to Longarm, and saw what Longarm saw.

He hardened his jaws and gave the lawman an incriminating glare. "Why, you . . . !"

"Hold on!" Longarm stared out the windows on the opposite side of the coach, which was now the ceiling. Fast hooves pounded, and tack squawked. A man was breathing raspily, eagerly, grunting softly.

Longarm looked around for his gun. Remembering he'd dropped his Colt out the window, he tried to find his rifle amidst the dust, gravel, and bodies littering what was now the bottom of the coach, noting absently in light of the continued danger that both the saddle tramp and the drummer were cruelly twisted and bloody, their lightless eyes staring.

The Winchester barrel poked out from beneath the drummer's left shoulder. Longarm gave a grunt, and brusquely tossing Raquella onto her husband, who howled painfully, he grabbed the rifle out from under the drummer. Hearing hoof thuds and spur chings growing louder, Longarm quickly but quietly racked a shell into the Winchester's breech.

"Señorita?" the half-breed called, his voice pitched with drunken mockery.

A tall, thick shadow fell over the side of the carriage to Longarm's left, where a large, ragged-edged panel had been torn off the coach's roof. A pair of tall, dusty black boots with silver Chihuahua spurs stopped just outside the opening. The half-breed bent down until his face appeared in the ragged hole. He held a silver-plated revolver in a black-gloved hand. He stretched his lips back from his brown teeth, grinning demonically.

"Señorita, are you okay in there?"

Raquella gasped.

The half-breed's eyes slid over to find Longarm's Winchester pointing at him.

"What about us fellas?" Longarm asked mildly.

The skin above the bridge of the cutthroat's nose wrinkled, and his jaw dropped as he swung his revolver toward the hole. He hadn't gotten his gun even halfway leveled, however, before Longarm punched a .44-40 slug through the middle of the man's tan forehead.

He hit the ground on his back.

His large-roweled spurs spun, shining like honey in the afternoon light.

Chapter 5

Longarm tossed the last shovelful of dirt on Eli Fischer's
mounded grave, stuck the spade's bit in the flinty ground,
and leaned on the handle, sweating. The sun was nearly
down, but it was still hot this close to the border, which he
could see from here, looking out through the saguaro-
stippled chaparral bathed in the pink light of early evening. Mexico was only a few miles away.

Someone sighed softly behind him. He turned to see
the girl, Raquella, near some paloverdes growing along a
dry wash. She must have come up behind him while he'd
been touching up the four graves he'd dug and laid the
driver, shotgun messenger, drummer, and saddle tramp in.

Raquella was holding a crucifix on a beaded silver
chain against her breasts, a black shawl around her shoulders. Her dress was dusty and torn, her hair disheveled.
Somehow, dirty and rumpled, she looked even more beautiful than she had before the wreck.

"Four good men dead," she whispered, her dark brown
eyes sliding across the graves over which Longarm had

mounded rocks to hold the predators at bay. "And all my fault."

Longarm shouldered the spade, which he'd found in the coach's jockey box under the driver's boot, and walked over to her. "You'd only wanted to stretch your legs and get a goddamn drink of water. The man whose fault this is lies over there, in that ravine I dragged him to. The coyotes are probably already givin' him his reckoning."

He glanced along the stage's back trail. Dark, winged specks circled over the trail in the western distance. "The *zopilates* have already found the other four." He glanced at Raquella still brooding over the graves. "How's your husband?"

She hiked a shoulder, and the shawl slid down to caress the inside curve of her tan right breast. "He is drinking his brandy, so he is feeling better." She looked up at Longarm. "I am brewing coffee. It is probably almost done. Would you like some, Señor Lang?"

"I could do with a cup."

Longarm couldn't help staring at her. He'd seen few women so intoxicating that they could mesmerize him even in the wake of watching several men die and enduring a violent stage coach crash. "And I reckon I might as well tell you now, since we're only a few miles from Santiago and you're bound to find out soon, anyway— the name ain't Lang. It's Long. Custis Long. I'm a deputy U.S. marshal out of Denver." Her black eyes probed his, and he found himself quirking a tender smile. "You can call me Longarm. Most folks do whether they like me or not."

He placed a light hand on her back. She allowed him to turn her around, still regarding him curiously, and they began walking back toward the camp they'd set up near the wreck and where her husband, Malcolm Mayfair, lay with a leg broken in two places. "I do not understand. A U.S. marshal?"

"I'm out here to pick up a prisoner the sheriff in Santiago is holding for me. I aim to take him back to Denver to answer charges there, in the federal court. I was using the phony handle and decked out in these saddle-tramp duds to throw certain folks off my trail—the coyotes that crashed the stage, anyways." Longarm gave a chuff, acknowledging the situation's grim irony. "Chain Link riders. The same men I was hoping to avoid."

"They are friends of the man in the jail in Santiago?"

"I don't know if you could call them friends, exactly." Longarm stepped down into the arroyo and turned automatically, extending his hand to Raquella. "But they ride for his pa, sure enough. And Norvell Wade is known for hiring tough riders. Pistoleers from both sides of the border."

"*Sí*. I have heard the name." She paused for a moment, glancing at Longarm's extended hand. She flushed slightly, gave him her soft, small, fine-boned hand with a large diamond wedding band on her ring finger. The touch shot lances of pleasure throughout Longarm's body, and he found himself keeping the girl's hand in his as he led her across the arroyo toward the deer path climbing the other side.

"You're from around here, then?"

"*Sí*. From just south of the border. A village called Aqua Norte. My father had a hacienda there, and the people from the town worked his fields until . . ."

Longarm looked at her as he helped her up the bank.

She was lifting her skirts above her ankles with one hand. They were damn fine ankles, tapering nicely to well-turned calves. When he had her standing beside him, he continued looking at her, one brow cocked, waiting for her to finish. She wore a sad, perplexed expression as she gazed off into the brush, as if looking for the words with which to finish her story.

"Until," she said finally, "banditos burned the rancho and most of the village, and killed my parents and my brother, Ubre."

"I'm sorry."

She looked down. Longarm followed her gaze to see that he was still holding her hand. Reluctantly, he released it.

They locked gazes for a moment. There was an awkward silence. Longarm felt his temples throb, his throat turn as dry as the arroyo they'd just crossed. Finally, he swallowed, held his hand out to indicate the path, and they started forward once more, Longarm letting her walk ahead of him.

"I take it you're lucky as well as fortunate to be alive," he said, eyes glued to the small of her slender back, shamelessly appreciating the erotic swell and sway of her hips as she walked.

"Father always kept a fast horse saddled for me in case of an attack by banditos or Apaches," Raquella said, keeping her head forward. "I took the horse and rode to my uncle's rancho. It was a long, grueling ride across the desert. But, as you say, Marshal Long"—she stopped at the edge of their camp, where her husband was sitting with his back against a sandstone wall—"I am fortunate to be alive."

"Your words say one thing," Longarm told her, standing just inches away from her. "The way you say them means another."

She seemed about to say something else. But then she shook her head slightly, turned away, and moved into the slight clearing in the rocks and piñons where the fire she'd built earlier had all but died, though tendrils of steam slithered up out of the black, rust-spotted coffeepot, which Longarm had also found in the jockey box.

Malcolm Mayfair sat on the other side of the fire. As Longarm approached the flames, he saw that the man's eyes were open, his brows beetled suspiciously.

"Where the hell have you two been?" he said in his heavy Southern accent, drawing out each word with suspicion.

"Marshal Long was burying the dead, Malcolm." Raquella dabbed at the man's sweat-beaded forehead with a damp cloth. "How is your leg?"

"It hurts." Mayfair stared at Longarm, who was pouring two cups of coffee, one for himself, one for the girl. "You sure that's all you were doin' out there?"

"Malcolm!" Raquella admonished. "That is no way to speak to a man who set your leg and quite possibly saved your life."

"I'm not so sure he set it right," the Southerner grunted, looking down at the swollen purple limb that Longarm had set with splints and strips of harness leather that had been left with the stage when the horses had torn away from the hitch. "He might have done more harm than good."

Longarm gave the man a cool look over his steaming coffee cup, holding his tongue.

"What's this 'Marshal Long' business?"

"It's a long story," Longarm quipped in a feeble attempt to lighten the mood.

Seeing it wasn't working, and not enjoying the Southerner's company half as much as his wife's, he threw back a couple of slugs of the terrible coffee—he had a feeling Raquella hadn't done much cooking on the rancho where she'd grown up—and threw the rest into the brush. Tossing the cup down on his saddlebags, which had been carried in the stage's luggage boot, he straightened and looked at Raquella still dabbing at her husband's sweat-beaded forehead.

"I'm gonna see if I can track a couple of the stage horses down. We'll use them to get to Santiago in the mornin'. I left the saddle tramp's pistol there." Longarm glanced at the old Remington revolver he'd set atop a rock. "If anyone comes, shoot twice in the air, and I'll be back to check 'em out before we let 'em into camp."

Raquella glanced at him knowingly. There were probably quite a few men out here who wouldn't mind having a go at such a creature as Mrs. Mayfair. "*Sí*," she said, and splashed more water onto the cloth wadded in her hand.

Longarm set his rifle on his shoulder and walked away.

After a long walk through the darkening desert, Longarm found his lost Colt as well as all six of the stage horses grazing contentedly in a box canyon fed by a spring dribbling down from a canyon wall and filling a broad pool around which galleta grass grew thick. A couple of the horses were skittish after the day's excitement and ran off as Longarm approached. The rest remained in the canyon and gave the lawman little trouble as he stripped their collars and hames and the rest of what remained of their tack after they'd broken away from the coach.

He fashioned crude halters from the dry, dusty reins, then dropped to his hands and knees and bathed his face in the pool, drinking deeply of the chill spring water. It was good dark by the time he returned to the Mayfairs, then used rope gleaned from the wrecked carriage to form a picket line for the horses.

"You found them!" Raquella intoned excitedly as he rubbed one of the horses down with a scrap of burlap he'd cut from a feed sack.

"Yes, ma'am. They weren't . . ." As he turned to where Raquella stood with her back to the fire, he let his voice trail off. Rather, it was clipped off as though he'd been punched in the belly and nearly driven to his knees.

She'd obviously found her luggage, and she'd changed into a nightdress with a sheer silk wrapper. The nightdress didn't amount to much more than the wrapper did, and, silhouetted as she was by the orange, snapping fire behind her, all that silk glowed softly. What was inside all that silk was clearly revealed—every curve and lump and upthrust of succulent female flesh.

She'd taken her hair down and brushed it, and it hung long and straight across her shoulders. As she stood there, staring at Longarm, holding a cup of steaming coffee in each hand, a bottle tucked under her arm, he could see her full, proud breasts rising and falling heavily.

Slowly, glancing shyly down, she came forward. She was wearing little silk slippers to protect her feet from the sharp gravel and wicked goatheads. The closer she came toward him, the better he was able to smell her. Obviously, she'd taken a sponge bath at the nearby spring and sprinkled herself with some subtle but sweet fragrance reminiscent of burning piñon and cherry blossoms.

Longarm's heart thudded as she drew so close he could feel the warmth of her body in the chill desert air, see the light shed by the quarter-moon sparkle in her eyes and glisten in her hair.

"Coffee?" she said just above a whisper.

He looked at the cup she held out to him, but his attention immediately traveled beyond it to her all-but-revealed, shadowy breasts pushing out the two layers of silk that did very little to cover them. Christ, she was as good as naked. So naked, in fact, he could see the nipples of those swollen orbs pebbling and jutting toward him.

Longarm cleared his throat. "Aren't you chilly, Mrs. Mayfair?"

"Just a little. But my blood is warm."

"Your husband asleep?"

"*Sí.* Sound asleep. He drank nearly an entire bottle of brandy." Coyly, Raquella cocked her head to one side and arched a brow. "Why?"

"Because suddenly I don't want any coffee."

She met his gaze boldly, the coffee steaming in her hands.

"What do you want, Marshal Long?"

"You know what I want, Mrs. Mayfair. What all men want when they're around you." Longarm plucked both cups from her hands, tossed them out into the brush, where they landed with a clink. He grabbed the girl's arms, drew her to him. "How deep does he sleep when he's had a snootful?"

She took a moment responding, ran her tongue across her upper lip. "Very, very deep."

Longarm drew her closer, pressed his lips to hers. She responded, opening her mouth for him, meeting his tongue with her own and wrapping her arms around his neck. He could feel her breasts swelling against his chest. His loins burned, his pants grew tight across his crotch.

After a time, he held her away from him. "I don't normally sleep with married gals, but I got a feelin' you two aren't all that married. Am I right about that?"

Raquella was nearly breathless as she sagged back in his arms. "He won me in a poker game . . . from my uncle."

"Had a feelin' it was something out of the general run of things. Didn't realize it was that far off the beaten path."

"He is not well, Marshal Long. The drinking . . . it has made him . . . unable to satisfy a woman."

Longarm gave a rueful chuff and hungrily ran his eyes across her heaving breasts. "Now, that I sorta suspected."

In spite of the hammering in his temples and the blood boiling in his veins, he glanced back toward the fire screened by the brush and a low rock pile. Silhouetted by the crackling and snapping fire, Mayfair slept with his back against the stone ridge. In spite of the man being an asshole, Longarm's conscience ached like a bad tooth. Raquella must have read it in his face.

She placed her hands on his face, gently turned his head back to hers. She said just barely loudly enough for him to hear, her raspy voice pitched with desperation, "I am not a whore, and I do not make a habit of lying with other men. But I would like, if for only one time in my life, to be made to feel like a woman, Marshal Long."

Another wave of hot passion stormed through Longarm. It soothed the ache in his conscience, and he pulled her to him once more, running his hands up the backs of her thighs and across her taut, round rump, caressing her through two layers of silk.

She moaned as she kissed him, running her hands across his broad shoulders, kneading them with the heels of her hands, sliding one soft leg between his and caressing his crotch with her knee. Longarm heard himself groan as he entangled his hot tongue with hers, the two of them making sucking sounds as they bit at each other's mouths and mashed their lips and groins together hungrily.

When she dropped a hand down and pressed it against the hard-on forming a long, thick bulge in the crotch of his pants, he nearly passed out. Suddenly, he bent down and picked her up in his arms. She gasped, clung to him desperately. He carried her over to his bedroll, which he'd spread near the picketed stage horses, intending to sleep away from the camp and the temptation of her. Holding her high against his chest, he suckled one of her breasts. She groaned and ran both her hands through his hair and nuzzled his neck; he could feel her wet lips and hot breath against his jawline, and it nearly drove him into a frenzy.

He dropped to his knees, laid her gently down on his soogan. She lay moaning and squirming around, staring up at him, her black eyes reflecting the moonlight like silver sparks flying from a grindstone. Quickly, breathing hard, he kicked out of his boots. Then he unbuttoned his shirt, tossed it down beside his saddle.

"Hurry, Marshal," Raquella rasped, reaching toward

him, spreading her legs as she rocked from side to side on her bottom.

Through the diaphanous silk, he could see the black V of her waiting crotch. Her raging need mixed with the other smells of her; it was like a hundred–proof firewater. Longarm's head reeled with it. He thought his pants would split before he could get them off.

Get them off he finally did, kicking them away with a curse. He slipped out of his socks, then peeled his long-handles down his arms, chest, and legs, his raging boner springing free—so hard that it ached. Seeing the jostling organ, Raquella gave a louder, animal-like groan and flung both her hands toward it.

"Give it to me!"

She scrambled up onto her knees. When she wrapped her hands around the organ in which all his nerve endings were firing like Peacemaker revolvers, Longarm nearly shot his full load. When he sat down against his saddle and she fondled and pumped him, sliding her nose across his love shaft's bulging purple head, he had to try doubly hard to control himself. Of course, he could just let himself go and start all over again, make a night of it between this queenly goddess's spread legs, her mouth, and the deep valley between her breasts, but he'd become accustomed to keeping himself on a leash as long as he could.

More fun that way.

Raquella moaned and groaned as she pumped him. Longarm sat back and closed his eyes. It was almost as though the girl had never seen a cock before, she seemed so taken with it, examining it closely so that he could feel her hair brushing across his balls and hips, tickling. She licked at it, pressed her fingers against it.

Then she whimpered and mewled and closed her mouth over the head, sucking it like a nickel lollipop. The wet crackling sounds along with the musky smell coming off of the lusty girl added to Longarm's torture.

When she started officially giving him a blow job, sliding her mouth as far down his pounding love handle as she could and then sliding it back up again, Longarm cursed and grabbed her arms. "That's enough there, girl."

Her lips came off his cock with a soft popping sound. She looked up at him, her swollen lips wet, eyes pouting. "Why?"

"'Cause it's time we went to it good and proper." Longarm pulled her up toward him, then shoved her down against his blankets. "Not that I mind French lessons, but I'm sort of a more traditional fella when it comes to the first round. Besides, I've been dreaming about burying my poker in your firebox for so long, I'm startin' to think I might just stroke out before I'm able to do it."

"*Mierda* . . . you're going to fuck me?"

Longarm chuckled. "Isn't that what you want?"

"I don't know." She snaked her arms around his neck and closed her mouth over his left shoulder, sinking her teeth in gently. "I'm afraid. What if I am not enough woman for you?"

Longarm looked down at her heaving breasts, both shadowy and milky with the moonlight snagging on the silk curtain of her wrapper falling away from them. He let his gaze trail down her flat belly to her spread legs, the dark V between them. The smell was stronger now. He placed his hand between her knees and up under the wrapper and nightgown, felt the hot, furry wetness.

The sensation was like a lightning bolt lancing them both; they shuddered as one.

Longarm swallowed down a thick knot in his throat and chuckled once more. "Oh, I think you'll be more than enough, Miss Raquella."

"Ohhhhh . . ." she cooed, chewing her fist while looking down at what he was doing with his hand.

When he was sure she was wet enough for him, the smell of fresh apricots wafting around him, enflaming him, he removed his hand, spread her legs wide, lifting them up high and out of the way with his forearms, and crabbed toward her on his knees. When he felt her furry, sopping snatch against the head of his cock, he grimaced as though a stiletto had pricked his heart.

She bit down hard on her fist and stared straight up at the moon, panting and chewing and trying hard not to cry out and possibly wake Malcolm.

"Oh," she growled softly, taking quick, darting glances down over her breasts to watch his long, hard shaft slide with excruciating slowness into the yawning mouth of her nest. "Oh . . . oooh . . . *siiiiiiit!*"

One of the horses nickered, and as Longarm bottomed out inside the girl, he glanced over his shoulder to see all three mounts staring back at him from their picket line.

"Mind your own business, ye damn perverts," he groaned as he began sliding out of her once more.

When he was almost entirely out, he thrust himself forward.

She sighed raspily into the hand that he was beginning to fear she'd chew completely off her arm before they were through, and then sort of mewled like a bobcat as he pulled out again. As he slid back in slowly, staying there longer than last time, rocking his hips around and grinding against her, grunting, she pressed her heels against the small of his back and began to buck.

She bobbed her hips gently at first, but by the time Longarm was going good, plunging in and out of her with the frenzy of a bronco stallion who hadn't fucked a prime mare in a month of Sonoran Desert Sundays, she was rising up to meet his every thrust, their thighs and bellies slapping together loudly. Longarm kept pushing her up against his saddle, and when her hair caught under it, he'd pause to drag her back toward him before resuming his frenzied toil between her bouncing knees.

Malcolm Mayfair coughed loudly from over by the fire. Raquella gasped with fright, and they stopped.

They turned their heads toward the bivouac. The Southerner coughed again, more softly, and rolled onto his side, pulling the blanket up tight against his neck. Longarm returned his fevered attention to the man's wife lying spread open before him, her skin glistening sweetly in the moonlight, and continued driving her closer and closer to the heights of carnal ecstasy, trying to time it just right so they'd meet there as one.

They did.

And Longarm had to clamp both his hands over her mouth to keep her scream from splitting the night wide open and waking her husband.

When they'd rested, watching the stars and fondling each other, she insisted on doing it again like the horses did it, with Longarm mounting her from behind. This time, he was slower, more passionate, nuzzling the back of the girl's pretty neck as he fucked her. She cooed and snorted and wagged her head like a mare.

"Oh, this . . . this I liiike, Marshal."

"Might as well call me Custis now, I reckon," he wheezed, squeezing her breasts as he pulled her hips back against him, slamming his cock up deep inside her once more.

"Oh, Custissssss . . ."

He sent them both off, finally, into a hard, deep, and dreamless sleep.

Chapter 6

"Oh, for cryin' in knee-high cotton! Marshal Long! Please! Must you ride so cotton-picking fast? You're nearly pulling this crazy contraption apart and rattling my teeth out of my jaws, not to mention causing a great disturbance in my *fucking leg!*"

Longarm hipped around on the bare back of the stage horse. He'd fashioned a travois of brush and branches for Malcolm Mayfair and strapped it to the one collar he'd salvaged from the wreck, using one set of stage ribbons.

He'd padded the travois with the dead saddle tramp's bedroll and even provided the Southerner with the pillow Eli Fischer had used to soften the coach's hard wooden driver's seat. The lawman had made the jury-rigged affair as comfortable as possible for the twelve-mile trek to Santiago. But the man had been complaining since the threesome, including the lovely Raquella, had pulled out of their camp late in the morning.

It was now midafternoon, shadows angling across the

endless maze of chaparral stretching off both sides of the
trail. Doves cooed and scrambled out from beneath mesquites as the three horses approached them, Longarm and
Raquella riding side by side, the travois scraping and
creaking along behind Longarm's bay gelding.

"If we ride any slower," Longarm told the Southerner,
"we won't be movin' at all."

Mayfair was craning his neck to peer over his shoulder and up at Longarm. He was hatless, dusty, and be-
draggled, his sandy hair in his eyes. "My leg throbs with
every bump in this miserable trail, and I'm out of brandy!"

"We're only a half mile from Santiago." Longarm
turned forward to peer along the stage trail snaking
through the saguaros and greasewood. "Bite down on
your hand, and we'll have you in a bed with a bottle and
a sawbones lookin' after your leg before you know it."

Raquella turned toward Longarm as she rode to his
left, a faintly incredulous look in her big, dark eyes.
Then he remembered her chomping down on her hand
last night while they'd frolicked amongst the mesquites,
and he felt his mouth corners shape a devilish grin. She
did likewise, eyes flashing in the sunlight, and turned to
look over her horse's bobbing head.

Longarm allowed himself a good look at her, riding
there beside him, tilted breasts bouncing pleasantly in
her bodice. She'd cut a long slit in her expensive riding
skirt, revealing almost the whole of her right leg. It was
long, golden, and shapely. She'd kicked out of her boots
before Longarm had helped her mount the horse after
their last water stop, and her bare foot had collected a
coating of dust. He figured she must have ridden horses
barefoot back on her father's rancho, and she was used
to riding this way. It gave her an alluring, rustic look,

and though he'd had her just a few hours ago, he wanted her all over again.

Something told him she was thinking the same thing. They had to be more careful if there was a next time, which didn't look likely since he wouldn't be in Santiago long. She and her husband would probably both be stuck in the town until Malcolm's leg mended, but Longarm would be riding out as soon as Buckshot Pete Peckinpah had turned over his prisoner to the federal lawman. Last night, Longarm and the girl had both fallen into such a deep sleep, entangled in each other's arms, that she'd barely made it back to her and her husband's camp before Mayfair had awakened, groaning melodramatically and complaining that he had to pee.

"Oh, God!" Mayfair intoned now. "Another bottle. What I wouldn't give for a drink right this instant!"

"Hush, Malcolm," Raquella gently chided her husband. "We'll be there soon and we'll get you all the brandy you can hold."

"Don't tell me to hush, goddamnit. The two of you were just lucky to make it through that gall-blasted wreck uninjured. If you only knew the pain I'm going through, riding along on this consarned confabulation!"

Longarm tuned out the rest of the man's grumbling. He also managed to partly tune out the presence of the man's lovely wife riding beside him, and turn his thoughts to what had brought him out here in the first place: Wesley Wade.

He wasn't sure how he was going to get the federal prisoner out of Santiago without a stagecoach. The one he'd been riding until yesterday had been scheduled to pull through Santiago, then swing north to the rail line another day beyond; it was on that coach he'd intended to hightail it with Norvell Wade's brigand son after the coach had laid over for a night in Santiago. He'd been hoping that Wade hadn't posted some men in town to make sure that Wesley and the stage did not leave together. Since Wade had had no idea when Longarm was arriving but had posted men on the stage trail east of Santiago, the rancher would have had no real reason to keep a close eye on the town.

But none of that mattered now.

It was doubtful the stage company had another coach in Santiago. They'd probably have to send another one out from Las Cruces, where the line originated. Now he'd probably have to rent a couple of horses and rough-trail Wade up to the rail line on his own. Which shouldn't be all that hard as long as the killer's father didn't get wind of a federal lawman's presence in Santiago. He'd heard the Wade ranch was nearly forty miles away, and if he could get young Wade out of town tonight after good dark, he'd likely be in the clear.

Not even the moccasin telegraph could cover forty miles that fast.

The only reason he hadn't wanted to rough-trail Wade on his own in the first place was simply because a stagecoach was faster, and he wasn't accustomed enough to this dry country to know where all the water holes were. Besides, Apaches were nearly always a threat out here.

"This is Santiago?" Raquella asked now as they descended a low, sandy hill. "I guess I thought it would be bigger, since it looked bigger on the map I saw in the last stage station."

"Just a dusty little border town," Longarm said. He'd been here for only a few hours once or twice in the past, hauling prisoners through. "It's the county seat, but I reckon it ain't much of a county. Probably only two or three big ranches. There were some gold and silver mines, but during the War when the Army boys were needed back East, the Mescaleros drove the prospectors out."

Norvell Wade's Chain Link was one of those two or three ranches, he thought, squinting ahead at the old Mexican shacks pushing up along both sides of the chalky trail. Keeping his hand close to the double-action Frontier Model Colt holstered for the cross-draw on his left hip, he kept his senses pricked for trouble.

There was an ancient ruined church that still boasted a bell in its adobe tower, goats grazing the brittle grass spiking up around its crumbling foundations. Around the church were chicken coops and pigpens, but most of the chickens and pigs appeared to be free ranging, snorting and clucking as they foraged in the chaparral.

"Oh, that smells pleasant," grumbled Mayfair as the horses crunched through several varieties of fresh dung in the road.

As they passed through the older, more haggard part of the town, where Longarm spied a girl suckling a baby on the stoop of her mud shack and the lonely strains of a guitar emanated from an unmarked, flat-roofed stone barrack that was apparently a cantina, the traffic picked up a bit. If you could call two slow-moving horseback-ers and three white women strolling the shaded board-walks "traffic." There were a couple of ranch wagons and surreys parked in front of false-fronted business establishments, including a mercantile and haberdash-ery. A couple of cow ponies stood hang-headed in front of a hotel that displayed the name RED RIDGE INN.

That was about it for the folks out and about. No signs of gun-hung, hawk-faced men lurking under outside stairwells or in alley mouths, watching for a federal lawdog.

It was just another quiet, hot, late-summer afternoon in Santiago with flies droning, an unseen blacksmith hammering an anvil, and a baby crying somewhere on the far side of town. A couple of comely girls skimpily clad in bright colors and feathers lounged on a second-floor balcony, Longarm saw as he and the Mayfairs followed a bend in the crooked street. Beneath them was a sign for a saloon, as well as a smaller one for DOCTOR LANCASTER HAINES, M.D. The saloon apparently took up the mud-brick, shake-shingled establishment's first story and part of its second story, while the doctor was housed in the far left side of the second floor, his door reached by an outside stairway that wasn't wearing its coat of green paint well in the Southwestern desert sun.

A saguaro cactus grew near the bottom of the steps, and a short-haired cur lounged in its shade, sleepily twitching its black ears at flies.

Longarm pulled up his horse in front of the saloon and looked up at the balcony. Both girls had come over to lean on the rail. They let their loose, low-cut shifts flop open, giving him a look at their wares as they smiled down at him.

"Hello, there," said the blonde, holding a half-smoked brown-paper cigarette in her right hand on the balcony rail. "What can we do you for you, big man?"

She slid her eyes toward Raquella as though wishing she weren't there. She took only passing notice of Mayfair, as though it was not unusual to see a man in an expensively cut albeit dusty suit dragged into Santiago on an Indian-style travois.

Longarm pinched his hat brim to both girls. "Ladies, is the doc in his digs over yonder?"

The brunette, who had red feathers in her short hair and whose small breasts were pushed up by the balcony rail, jerked her head to indicate behind her. "Not over yonder. In here. You want I should call him?"

"Oh, good Lord," Mayfair groused, dropping his hands down alongside the travois in disgust. "A whoremongering sawbones!"

Both whores frowned indignantly down at the Southern dandy.

Raquella chided him with, "Malcolm, shush!"

Longarm said to the girls, "If you wouldn't mind. In the meantime, we'll haul my friend here over to the Red Ridge Inn, get him a room. Once he's more comfortable, maybe he'll start mindin' his manners."

"Once he's more comfortable," said the brunette, leaning a little farther over the rail so that her pert breasts bulged a little higher, "why don't you come on over and take a load off"—she slid her eyes to Raquella—"less'n she's yours."

Longarm glanced at Raquella, who flushed and turned uncomfortably away. Longarm chuckled, feeling his own ears warm with embarrassment. "Oh, no, this one here is all hitched up to that one back there. And I'd likely be right over, but I got business that needs tendin'. Maybe later this evenin', Miss, uh . . ."

"Sharlane. And you come on over anytime and we'll share a bottle, big man."

"Maybe we'll both share a bottle with you, mister." The blonde grinned devilishly and wagged the string of fake pearls dangling over her billowy green satin shift.

Longarm pinched his hat brim to the blonde, then swung his horse back into the street and gigged it forward.

The two whores were comely for this far off the beaten desert path. Longarm didn't normally seek out whores for his bedroom entertainment, but since they'd sent out the invitation, he might well have considered obliging them for a good postsundown ash-hauling. But he'd need a good night's rest before lighting out with his prisoner first thing in the morning.

Behind him, Malcolm Mayfair called to the girls, "Send someone over with a bottle, uh ... ladies. I'll make it worth their time and effort!"

"If you say so, stranger," said the blonde without enthusiasm, her voice dwindling as Longarm pulled Mayfair around another bend in the street, Raquella riding stiff-backed ahead of him, her disapproval at his conversation with the pleasure girls obvious in the square set of her shoulders.

Longarm gave an ironic chuff. You'd think that just because they'd sweated and grunted around together for a couple hours, he belonged to her. Women.

He pulled up in front of the Red Ridge Inn, a simple, three-story sandstone building with a large false wooden front painted green but announcing its name in large red letters. The hotel was named after the high red sandstone ridge that loomed over the town from the northwest and at the bottom of which Santiago Creek meandered. He slid down from the stage horse's broad back and walked back to the travois to look down at Mayfair's dusty countenance.

The dandy looked sunburned and miserable. He spit dust from his lips and blinked it from his eyelashes.

"Thank God. I thought I was going to die before we ever made it to civilization." Mayfair shoved up on his elbows to look around the wide, all-but-deserted street sheathed in crude wooden, sandstone, or adobe brick business buildings. The shops and offices all looked sun-bleached and dusty, their brush arbors shading the occa-sional silhouetted townsman loafing on a plank bench or a wicker chair.

"If this is what serves as civilization out here . . ." Mayfield continued, grumbling and turning his mouth corners down in disgust.

"Tell me, Mayfair," Longarm said, scowling down at the man, having had enough of the man's holier-than-thou attitude, "if you hate it so much out here, why come?"

He'd been so taken by Raquella that he'd never learned where they were heading or why.

"We're on the way to Tucson," Mayfair said, scowl-ing up at Longarm. "And it's rather hard not to travel such a route from New Orleans, where I'm currently based, without enduring some of the ass-ugliest country populated by the most uncivilized of desert snakes in the Northern Hemisphere." He extended his arm to Long-arm and effortlessly switched his expression from bald disdain to beseeching. "Help me up?"

Longarm gave another ironic chuff as he took the man's right arm while Raquella, avoiding Longarm's gaze as she continued her snit, draped her husband's left arm around her neck. After enduring his complaining and groaning and muttered curses, they had him up on his good foot and were gently hauling him up to the Red Ridge Inn's raised veranda, Mayfair wheezing and suck-ing his lower lip with each step, like a five-year-old whom some bigger kid had relieved of his candy.

When he'd finally gotten the Mayfairs registered and into their room and had dropped Malcolm onto his bed, Longarm was as relieved as though he'd just outrun a passel of howling Lipan Apaches and saved his topknot by a hairsbreadth.

"Now, then," he said with a sigh. "I reckon I'll get on about my chores."

"Chores?" Raquella wanted to know, arching a brow at him. "Or whores? Those two *putas* seem to have taken an instant liking to you."

"Business before pleasure, Mrs. Mayfair." Longarm pinched his hat brim to her and headed for the open door.

He turned to look behind at Mayfair lying flat on his back with his splintered leg propped on a pillow, staring at the ceiling and muttering, "Brandy. Brandy. For God's sake—*brandy!*"

Longarm glanced at Raquella. "I'll stop back to check on things before I leave town."

Giving him a surprised, troubled look, she followed him into the hall, drawing the room's door partway closed behind her. "Leaving?"

"I told you—I'm here to pick up a prisoner and mosey. And, uh . . ." Longarm looked up and down the hall then added, keeping his voice down. "I'd appreciate it if you didn't spread that around."

"Who would I spread it to?"

Longarm turned and once more started down the hall. Once more, she called to him. "Custis?" She winced at the unintended loudness of her voice, and glanced at the door before turning back to him, a faint look of desperation and beseeching in her gaze.

He returned the look with a genuinely frustrated one

of his own. He'd like nothing better than to spend another night or two with the woman. But he had a man to see about a prisoner. He strode back to her, grabbed her around the waist, and kissed her.

"Maybe see you again sometime, Mrs. Mayfair."

"Good luck, Custis."

He walked away.

Chapter 7

Longarm made his way down to the carpeted lobby of the Red Ridge Inn to find the proprietor of the place, a short Mexican in a string tie and with thick, black hair combed with shiny pomade, standing behind the desk with a woman about his age, early forties. She was pretty in a big-bosomed, matronly way, and also dressed for business in a pink basque and with a string of pearls around her neck, silver loop rings hanging from her ears. Longarm had learned their names were Hector and Carlotta Padilla, and they both stopped arguing in hushed, quick Spanish to anxiously regard the tall stranger now in their lobby.

"Por favor, señor," said Hector, striding nervously out from behind the desk. "My wife doesn't believe me. You told me that the stage was not only attacked but *destroyed*—is that not so?"

Longarm stopped in front of the door to light a nickel cheroot with a stove match he'd flicked to life on his thumbnail. "'Fraid it's true. Fischer and his shotgunner are dead, along with a drummer and a saddle tramp whose name I have on a gun receipt. Not that it'll do any good. We can likely contact the drummer's next of kin through the company he worked for, but locating the saddle tramp's family might be a touch harder. I'll talk to the sheriff about it."

Padilla turned to prattle off some enervated Spanish at his wife, who returned it, throwing out her hands. Longarm wasn't sure what they were most concerned about—the loss of life or the loss of business they'd likely been counting on when the stage pulled into town. He drew deep on the cigar and pushed out through the hotel's door, nearly flattening a short, stocky gent in a bowler hat who was carrying a black accordion bag.

"Good Lord!" the man intoned, eyeing Longarm through thick spectacles that made his drink-bleary eyes look as large as coffee saucers.

Longarm grabbed the man's gravy-stained lapel to steady him, and glanced at the bag in his bony fist. "You the sawbones?"

"I am." He looked indignant at having been called away from a far more comfortable situation up the street a ways. His breath was sour and malty. "Dr. Lancaster Haines. The girls said I had a patient over here." He lifted a loosely-rolled, half-smoked quirley in his free hand, and took a deep drag. "I hope they can pay with something besides chickens and goats. I've grown right bored with my suppers of late!"

"You might just be eatin' a T-bone tonight, Doc. Upstairs yonder. Room nine."

With that, Longarm left the doctor scowling curiously after him as he descended the veranda steps and headed out into the quiet street, tramping through the well-churned dust and manure that puffed up around his ankles. He remembered that the sheriff's office and jailhouse was on the far western edge of Santiago, and that's where he found the bulky stone structure with a good-sized, roof-covered veranda and a stout wooden door. The door had a small, barred window shuttered from the inside.

There wasn't much out here but a single cantina that sat hunched and silent on the opposite side of the street and several dilapidated old warehouses moldering amongst the rocks, barrel cactus, and saguaros. On the jailhouse veranda, a slender figure in blue denims, red calico shirt, and brown leather vest was sitting kicked back in a chair. A five-pointed silver star was pinned to the man's vest. He had his boots crossed on the porch rail and his funnel-brimmed hat pulled down low over his eyes, chin dipped to his chest.

A sleeping deputy.

Since the man had a Winchester Yellowboy repeater resting across his thighs, the federal lawman walked up the porch slowly, not wanting to make any loud or sudden noises and risk getting himself ventilated. The deputies in these little jerkwater towns were often wannabe gunslicks, and you had to step careful around them or end up a notch on their pistol grips. He was about to clear his throat, but held silent. Something about the man had caught his attention—namely the bulge in the man's shirt behind the open vest and deputy sheriff's star. He let his eyes travel lower. The "man's" hips swelled invitingly.

Suddenly, the girl's head came up, her eyes flashing wide. As she started to jerk the rifle up, Longarm instinctively grabbed the carbine by its barrel and pulled it out of her hands. The girl gasped as she reached for the gun, but Longarm held it beyond her reach.

Fear shone in her hazel, almond-shaped eyes, and a flush rose in her smooth, tan, perfectly shaped cheeks as she heaved up out of her chair. "Hey, give me that, you son of a bitch!"

"Hold on, miss," Longarm said around the cigar in his teeth, stepping back and holding the rifle and his free hand out in supplication. "I just saw you start to waken mighty fast and instead of gettin' shot, I decided to grab the carbine. An impulsive move that I hope you'll forgive me for, but one stemming from too many years of getting shot at. Here, it's yours as long as you don't shoot me. I'm the deputy U.S. marshal out of Denver that Sheriff Buckshot Peckinpah has been waitin' for."

He held the rifle out to the girl, who grabbed it, lips angrily pursed. Her brows were the same tawny color as her hair, which tumbled down her shoulders in thick, alluring swirls. Her bosom rose and fell sharply behind the shirt and vest, making the deputy sheriff's star bob. Slowly, the anger left the lovely girl's hazel eyes, and she took Longarm's measure, raking him up and down.

"So, you're the federal."

"That's right."

She tipped her hat back to look up at him. "Kinda tall, ain't ya?"

"Same height I was yesterday." Since the girl was giving him the close study, Longarm returned the favor. It was fun. "Peckinpah hire you?" he asked with a laugh.

"No, he never hired me. And what're you laughing at? I can deputy as well as any of the men around here. Better, probably, 'cause I ain't the yellow-livered dogs they are. Fact is, Pa's down with the bottle flu, and I'm the only one I could get to pin the badge on my shirt."

Longarm smiled. "Pshaw. There must be one man around here who could help you with that."

"You know what I mean!"

"I reckon I do, but it's been a long ride. The stage was attacked, and the driver, shotgunner, and three passengers are dead. The only two survivors besides myself are over at the Red Ridge Inn. One's bein' tended by the medico."

The girl looked only mildly shocked as she rested the barrel of her rifle on her shoulder. "They got Fischer and Lonnie Beachum?"

Longarm flicked his cigar stub over his shoulder and into the street. "'Fraid so."

"Who?"

"Chain Link riders. Speaking of whom . . ." Longarm turned to flip the door latch and walk into the jailhouse.

"Hold on, there, Marshal . . ."

Longarm stepped over the threshold, the old smells of coffee, tobacco, and wood smoke as well as sweat wafting against him. The room also smelled of rock, of which it was solidly constructed. "Long," he finished for the girl. "Custis Long. You can call me Longarm. Most folks do."

He cast his gaze to the back of the fifty-by-fifty-foot jailhouse, where four cells were lined up, all with their doors closed. It was too dark in the barracklike place to see inside the cells, so he moseyed across the starkly furnished room, avoiding the single stove and the desk to his right that was fronting a wall map of Arizona Territory, toward the back.

The girl followed him into the building, stopping a few feet in front of the door. When Longarm had walked up for a close inspection of all four cells, finding nothing inside but made cots and empty slop buckets, he wheeled to the girl who stood, one hip cocked, rifle on her shoulder, staring at him grimly.

"Wade ain't here," she said. "That's why I was gonna say it was kinda strange you was run down by Chain Link boys."

Longarm pitched his voice with authority. "I reckon you'd best tell me where he is. I hope no farther than the privy, and, if he's out there he'd better be carrying an iron ball that's chained to both his murderin' ankles!"

"I'm sorry. That ain't how it is."

Longarm felt his ears warm with exasperation. "How the hell is it?" Before she could answer, he nearly shouted, "And where the hell is your pa? I don't care if he's got the hangover of a dozen Texas-to-Abilene drovers, I want to talk this over with Buckshot Pete himself."

"Pa's over at the Red Ridge Inn."

"What the hell's he doin' over there?"

"He lost our house in a crap game, so he . . . we . . . live there now, when he's not sleepin' off his hangovers here at his desk."

Longarm had started striding toward the front door but stopped to stare down at the girl. She looked away from him, her high cheeks coloring shamefully.

He wasn't sure why, but he suddenly found himself feeling vaguely sorry for her. He also felt the need to probe her a little more before stomping over to Pete Peckinpah's room and inquiring with the sheriff himself.

None of what he'd heard so far sounded anything like

the Buckshot Pete he knew. *Releasing a prisoner when he knew Longarm was on his way to pick the killer up to escort him to the hangman?*

"Buckshot Pete lost his . . . your . . . house in a crap game?"

She turned to stare at him sadly. "I got me a feelin', Longarm, that my father ain't exactly the same Buckshot Pete Peckinpah you once knew."

"Apparently not. Why'd he release Wesley Wade?"

"He didn't release him. Chain Link riders sprung him night before last, when my father was passed out drunk in one of the cantinas. Just waltzed right in, waved guns in the face of Pa's deputy, Everett Mills, and took him out. Oh, it wasn't Everett's fault. Everett's no lawman. He was just helping out. Pa never shoulda left an old man here alone while he went off to get drunk."

Longarm scowled in disbelief at the girl. "You're right, Miss . . ."

"Jessie."

"You're right, Miss Jessie. I'm havin' a hard time wrappin' my mind around such a story. I knew Buckshot Pete could drink his fill of hooch, but what in tarnation turned him into a lush?"

"What else, Longarm?" Jessie Peckinpah tapped her foot. "Cooch."

Longarm wagged his head slowly. "Musta been one helluva woman." He walked around the girl to the door. "I'm gonna go over and talk to your pa."

"Won't do you no good. He was out late last night. Likely won't wake till six, seven or so . . . then get up to start all over again. Lettin' Wesley Wade go was sorta the nail in Pa's coffin, so to speak. It busted him good, knowin' he did such a thing, and the only way he can escape it is crawlin' right back inside the same bottle that caused it."

"We'll see about that."

Longarm strode down off the jailhouse veranda and started back toward the Red Ridge Inn. It was getting late in the afternoon, the light softening, shadows lengthening. He noted several riders heading into town—Mexicans as well as gringos, all looking dusty and worn and sun-burned from another day's work on the ranches and ranchos in the area. Likely heading for the saloons and cantinas to stomp with their tails up.

He was only vaguely aware of the street. His mind was on Buckshot Pete and Wesley Wade. If Wade had been set free, the Chain Link riders who'd run the stage down must have been at the stage station only to wet their whistles. They hadn't been waiting for Longarm at all . . .

He slowed as a couple of wooly-looking horseback-ers rode out of an alley mouth. They started to cross the street in front of him, heading for a cantina on the street's other side. One turned toward him, turned away, then turned back quickly.

He was a big gringo in a felt sombrero, long sandy hair hanging down past his shoulders. He was dressed in both Mexican and American garb, including a short charro jacket over an elaborately embroidered collarless shirt, with large-roweled spurs on his black high-heeled boots. His face looked like a map of the Sonoran Desert, deeply lined and pink contrasting the bleached-out sandy beard.

His pale blue eyes narrowed as they took Longarm's measure, then flickered suddenly in recognition. The man grinned, lips spreading back from a silver eyetooth that flashed in the late sunlight.

Longarm's mind riffled through the names and faces filed randomly in the back of his head and coughed up a handle: Arroyo Simms. The man had three brothers, and they'd been running guns to the Comanche in West Texas until Longarm had gone down there and killed all three brothers in a two-day gun battle but somehow lost the oldest of the Simms bunch, Arroyo, in the Big Bend country.

Here he was now, looking a little older, some wilier, and a whole lot meaner.

"How-do, Longarm?" Simms said with a mocking laugh, pinching his hat brim to the federal badge toter. His other hand caressed the bone grips of the big Schofield revolver positioned for the cross-draw on his left hip.

He tossed his head toward the cantina he'd been heading for, his short Mexican partner sitting a desert barb on his other side. "Buy you a drink?"

"Maybe some other time, Simms."

"All right." Simms chuckled. The eyetooth flashed again. "I'll be around. I ride for the Chain Link, don't ya know!"

He winked, glanced at his partner, and booted his big Appaloosa on across the street.

Longarm glowered at the man's back, feeling a knot of tension tighten just beneath his belly button. Just how large a snakes' nest had he ridden into here in Santiago, anyway?

Chapter 8

"Which room is Sheriff Buckshot Pete Peckinpah snorin' off his coffin varnish in?" Longarm inquired of Hector Padilla, who was down on one knee and polishing the front of his ornately scrolled mahogany desk.

The head of a desert ram stared down over the desk as though in mild reproof at Longarm's query. A clock ticked on the finely papered lobby wall opposite, while a low hum of conversation emanated from the open double glass doors that apparently led to the hotel's bar and dining room. Longarm thought he also detected the snick of pasteboards.

Evening was starting in Santiago.

"Room twelve, señor," Padilla said in his thick Mexican accent, looking up and over his left shoulder at the tall federal lawman. "But it will do no good to call on him yet, señor. He did not retire until nearly noon today, which means he will likely not stir again until nine o'clock tonight at the earliest."

"We'll see about that!"

Longarm swung around and headed up the carpeted stairs. On the second floor landing, he almost ran into the doctor, who gave a start at the tall man tramping up the stairs two steps at a time, and held his medical kit before him as though for protection.

"How's Mayfair, Doc?" Longarm said, pausing.

"The broken bones seem to have been set adequately. I'm told by Mrs. Mayfair that you're responsible for that." The doctor canted his head and narrowed one eye curiously. "Who are you, anyway? You seem to carry more authority on your shoulders than the average saddle tramp you're dressed like."

"I'm nobody, Doc. Just passin' through."

Longarm started down the second floor hallway, the deep red carpet muffling the thuds of his low-heeled cavalry boots but not keeping the floorboards from squawking. He passed the Mayfairs' closed door and continued to the door identified by a brass number twelve. Leaning his head close to listen through the door panels, he heard deep, raucous snoring.

Chuffing his disgust, he rapped the door three times hard—*boom! boom! boom!*—and waited.

There was a woman's sigh. The man's loud snoring continued.

Again, Longarm chuffed. He twisted the doorknob. The latch clicked. The fool had probably been too soused to lock it when he'd finally gone to bed.

Throwing the door wide, the lawman stomped into the room and stopped at the foot of a canopied bed on the room's right side. Pete Peckinpah lay buck naked on his back, both arms thrown straight out from his shoulders, one resting at an angle across the back of the young woman sprawled belly down beside him, her hair looking like a giant red beehive spilled across her pillow.

She was a pale girl with a nicely rounded rump, Longarm absently noted as he strode over to the washstand straight ahead of him and grabbed a nearly full water pitcher from its porcelain bowl. He took the pitcher over to the bed, waited for Buckshot Pete's mouth to open once more, loosing a resonating snore, then splashed the entire contents of the pitcher into the sheriff's bearded face.

Bellowing like a poleaxed bull, Buckshot Pete Peckinpaw bolted straight up in bed, eyes and mouth wide and shaking the water from his face and thick, matted, gray-streaked hair. "Who in the holy livin' hell just done that? I'll kill the motherfuckin' son of a two-peso whore!"

At the same time, the girl—likely, a sporting girl—lifted her own head from her pillow and twisted around on the bed, looking sleepily indignant as she brushed droplets from her pale, slender, lightly freckled shoulder. "Hey—what's the big idea?"

Longarm let the pitcher hang slack in his right hand. "It's Custis, Pete." He waved a hand in front of the man's eyes, for the Santiago sheriff seemed to be staring straight across the room at nothing. "Custis Long out of Denver's First District Federal Court. Longarm, for short. Remember? I was sent here to pick up Wesley Wade."

Only at the mention of Wade did the sheriff's mud brown eyes acquire a spark of recognition. He swung his dripping head toward Longarm and, running a hand across his sopping beard, narrowed his eyes at the federal lawman towering over him. "Wade?" He blinked. Then he scowled. "Ah, shit, Custis."

"What happened, Pete?"

"They busted him out."

"I heard that much from your daughter."

"Well, then, hell, Custis," Peckinpaw said, turning away from Longarm and snuggling back down against his now-soaked pillow, "what the hell you botherin' me about?"

He smacked his lips, drew a deep breath, and let it out.

"Yeah, what're you botherin' him about?" the sporting girl moaned, lifting her knees and crossing her arms over her ample, pale, lightly freckled breasts. "Why don't you just hightail it out of here, mister, and let us sleep? We had a long, hard night."

"Looks that way." Longarm looked at Peckinpaw, who, curled up beside the girl, was snoring loudly once more. "When him and you wake up, miss, you can tell Buckshot Pete he's no longer the sheriff of Santiago County."

"Oh, yeah?" the girl snapped, giving him the indignant twice-over with her light brown eyes. "Who is?"

"His daughter—that's who."

With that, Longarm wheeled away from the bed and headed out the door, slamming it loudly behind him.

"Fuck you, too!" the sporting girl screeched.

Longarm stopped in the hall. Peckinpah's daughter stood before him, leaning against the opposite wall, looking glum, one boot hooked over the other. She was leaning on her rifle, the barrel of which was snugged against the carpeted floor.

"Didn't do you much good, did it?"

Longarm poked his hat brim off his forehead. He was sorry that the girl had heard him fire her father, but she would have learned about it sooner or later. Especially when he told her she'd be wearing the sheriff's badge until he could seat someone else and until the town council could hold a formal meeting and run an election.

"No, I reckon it didn't." The federal lawman shook his head and hooked a thumb at the door behind him. "How long's he been like that?"

"Almost a year now. Ever since Spring left him two days before they was supposed to get hitched and made him the laughingstock of the town. What those folks forgot, though, was how Pa came here and cleaned out the riffraff. What he couldn't clean out he sent to Boot Hill. That's why, in the year Pa's been wet-nursin' and cantina crawlin', there ain't been much trouble. Till he arrested Wesley Wade, that is. Caught Wade even drunker than Pa in the Sonora Saloon; otherwise, he likely wouldn't have been able to haul him in without a posse."

"I'm surprised he arrested that killer in the first place, if he's been this bad."

"When he heard there was a federal warrant on him out of Denver, he figured you'd be coming for him. I think Pa wanted to put on a good show for you. He did . . . for a while. Kept Wade under lock and key, guarded the jail himself, sent me out on patrols." Jessie sighed and let her hand drop against her thigh. "Then he fell back in the bottle."

Again, Longarm shook his head, still unable to wrap his mind around the drunkard Buckshot Pete had let himself become. Turning, he started tramping down the hall. Jessie fell into step beside him.

"What's on your plate now, Longarm?"

"Well, first thing I'm gonna do is get Wesley Wade back under lock and key. Can you recommend a livery stable where I might be able to find a fast horse?"

"You're gonna go now—today? Hell, it'll be dark in a couple hours."

Longarm glanced out the window on the second floor landing. "Shit."

"Best wait till tomorrow," Jessie said as she and Longarm dropped down into the lobby. "I'll take you out there, if you want."

Longarm stopped and looked at her, one brow raised.

"I'm not scared of them Wades," she said, shaking loose strands of her rich, tawny hair back from her suntanned cheeks.

"I can see you got your father's gravel. Back when he *had* gravel, that is."

"He's still got it, Longarm. I'm just waitin' for him to find it again. I think he is, too."

Longarm glanced at the clock ticking on the lobby's red-papered wall, just above the varnished cherry wainscoting. "Well, since I won't be leaving town till tomorrow, I might as well have a drink and a meal, then see the Padillas about getting a room. Think I'll bunk here, since everyone else is," he added wryly.

He turned back to Jessie and allowed himself a short but enjoyable glance at her body, all the curves of which were wonderfully revealed and complemented by her tight, faded denims—the cuffs of which she wore tucked inside her worn, brown, mule-eared boots—and the men's wool shirt that was pulled taut against her proud bosoms. "Join me for supper, or at least a drink, Miss Peckinpah? Or you got a young man waiting on your company?"

She saw the mannish look he'd favored her with, and her tan cheeks colored a little. She looked away, and Longarm suddenly realized that, despite her rugged, brash demeanor, deep down she was shy. "There's no young man waitin' for me, Longarm. I reckon I haven't run into the right one yet, or he hasn't run into me. I'll take that drink offer, but I'd best save supper for later. I have to start makin' my rounds in a half hour."

Longarm led Jessie to a corner table in the dining room, a good distance from the crowd gathering up around the bar and near the roulette wheel and faro lay-out. Longarm wanted the separation so he could keep an eye on things. He noted that Jessie sat with her back to a wall, as he did, and he smiled to himself. The girl had inherited her father's lawman's instincts . . . when old Pete had still *had* instincts, that is.

When Longarm had looked over the nicely appointed dining room and had spied no others like Arroyo Simms who might be gunning for him, he caught the eye of the chubby young Mexican waitress—likely a Padilla daughter—and ordered a Maryland rye for himself. To his surprise, Jessie ordered a straight shot of bourbon.

But why was he surprised? If he remembered correctly, bourbon was the drink of choice for Buckshot Pete.

Jessie doffed her hat, tossed it onto the table. She didn't seem to care that it left her hair disheveled around her shoulders, partly hanging in her eyes. Leaning forward, she picked up her shot glass between the thumb and index finger of her right hand and tossed back half the shot.

She swallowed, winced a little, a pleased cast entering her hazel eyes, then sank back in her chair, puffing her cheeks out with a weary sigh. "To tell the truth, Longarm," she said, "bein' the drunken sheriff's daughter don't make me real popular. I did have me a beau from one of the ranches out yonder, and we was sparkin' along just fine until Pa pulled his gettin' drunk and being useless stunt. That's when Roy decided to start calling on a girl from one of the other ranches instead."

"Roy's loss."

"That's also about when I started takin' over for Pa regular. That's not too popular with the menfolk, either—a girl with a badge. They like law and order and all, and so far I'm managin' to keep the peace even after midnight, but it somehow seems to offend the men of Santiago. Offends 'em even more when I tell 'em I'd be right happy to turn the badge over to one of their cowardly asses!"

Jessie chuffed a caustic laugh, then leaned forward to throw back the rest of her shot.

"Why's the job so unpopular?" Longarm asked, throwing back his rye and signaling the waitress to bring them each two more. It appeared Jessie could keep up with him without much trouble.

Jessie hiked a shoulder. "I reckon there's just other jobs that pay better out here. And no one wants to prance around the Mex cantina after, say, nine o'clock. That's when we get a bad element in Santiago. Border toughs and out-an'-out owlhoots, most likely wanted south of the border or over in California. I don't mind admittin' "—she gave Longarm a sincere look, her eyes only slightly clouded by the bourbon—"I've been right lucky so far. 'Pears the mangiest cutthroat border snake balks at shootin' a girl, even one wearin' a badge." She laughed and took a dainty sip of her second shot, which the bar girl had just set down in front of her. "That hesitation planted two of 'em on Boot Hill, both with slugs from my Winchester through their black hearts."

Digging into his shirt pocket for a fresh cheroot, Longarm stared at the girl in amazement.

"I'd have gone out to arrest Wesley Wade my own self—after Pa let him go—but I figured I'd be pushing my luck bucking the entire Chain Link crew. I'm not sure how you're gonna handle *that* one, Longarm. Maybe you oughta wire Fort Huachuca for help from the bluecoats."

"If I wired the army for help, I'd be here till next spring, waiting on 'em." Longarm scraped a stove match to life with his thumbnail. "Since I reckon I'll be ridin' out there solo, I'll have to find a way to cut that loco wolf out of his pack." Puffing smoke, he rolled a glance to the girl, who was staring down at her half-empty shot glass. "Any ideas?"

"Like I told you, I'll back your play out there."

Longarm shook his head. "No, thanks. You're needed here in Santiago. Besides, I work best alone."

"One o' them, huh?"

"I reckon."

"Well, the best way to get Wesley away from his pa and the other men—at least most of the other men—is to corral him over at the Pantera Cantina in Piñon Canyon, about five miles south of the border. I'm told he can usually be found there at night after about nine o'clock. His pa don't want him leaving the Chain Link, but after the old man turns in, Wesley sneaks away with a couple of his amigos to romp with the cantina's whores. He's got him a special one, I hear. One he prefers above all others and has pretty much made his own, threatening to slit her throat if she dallies. A real charmer, don't ya know."

Longarm inhaled a lungful of tobacco smoke and let it out slowly through his nostrils, several pensive creases marring his leathery forehead. "Good information, Jessie. Damn good information. If he always shows up at the same spot at the same time, without too many other gents backing him . . ."

"Only problem," Jessie said pointedly, "is you'll be crossing Chain Link graze on the way there and back. Norvell Wade always keeps pickets posted here and there about his spread, to keep rustlers and nesters out, and you never know where you're gonna find 'em."

"How long does Wade usually stay at the Pantera?"

"Till two or three in the morning. Sometimes later, depending how good a poker game he's involved in . . . or how drunk he's gotten."

"How long will it take me to ride out there?"

"Four, five hours from Santiago."

"All right, then—I'll leave before dark so I'm crossing the Chain Link graze at night. If all goes well, I should have the little hookworm back here under lock and key by sunrise the next day."

"If all goes well."

Longarm lifted his shot glass to the girl. "Here's to all go . . ."

He let his voice trail off when he saw Raquella Mayfair stroll through the dining room's double doors and head for the bar. The muscles in the back of Longarm's neck tensed automatically, and he was about to be grateful that she hadn't seen him when she glanced toward his and Jessie's table, and she saw him.

She stopped suddenly and smiled, swinging her body around to face him. But the corners of her mouth leveled out and her eyes grew chill as they slid between Longarm and Jessie. The federal lawman's loins turned cool as gravestones. If that wasn't a look of jealousy sweeping Raquella's face, Longarm was a hook-handed stevedore working the docks of San Francisco with a cod-loaded clipper ship creaking against her watery stays.

Arching a brow, squaring her shoulders, and crossing her arms over her breasts, the beautiful Mexican strolled toward his and Jessie's table, Raquella's stygian hair shining in the light from the hissing gas lamps.

Chapter 9

Longarm swallowed the tight knot in his throat and set his shot glass down on the table as Raquella walked up to it, furling a brow at him and Jessie like a nun who'd caught two mission school students passing dirty notes when they should have been copying their day's catechism.

"Señor Long," the striking Mexican beauty said softly, "I see you have already found a friend here in Santiago."

Longarm glanced at Jessie, who returned the look as she slowly set her own shot of bourbon down. The lawman scraped his chair back and stood, lifting his mustache with a taut smile as he said, "Raquella Mayfair, this is Jessie Peckinpah—Buckshot Pete's daughter and deputy sheriff of Santiago. Jessie and me was just sittin' here over drinks discussin' business."

He opened his hand toward a free chair. "But, please, sit down. Looks like you and Malcolm will be here awhile, him on the mend an' all. Might as well get acquainted with the local law first thing."

He chuckled, sounding like a fool even to himself. Throughout his career, he'd faced many a devil-eyed killer without batting a lash, but for some reason a woman's chill glance could make him piss a cold stream down his pants leg.

"You were on the stage?" Jessie asked Raquella.

"*Sí*. It was terrible—so many killed. We, too—my husband and I," Raquella added a shade guiltily, "would certainly have been murdered as well if not for Marshal Long's quick thinking and blazing guns."

Longarm's ears warmed as he stood awkwardly at the table beside Jessie. Raquella wore a black wool shawl across her bare shoulders. She'd been holding the garment closed when she'd entered the saloon, and he didn't know if she'd released it to torment him on purpose, but it was open now, the ends hanging down her arms, exposing her swollen tan cleavage in which nestled her small, jade-set crucifix.

"Quick thinkin' and blazin' guns," Jessie said, whistling softly and looking up at Longarm with faint mockery in her bright hazel gaze. "Sounds like he saved your bacon all right, Mrs. Mayfair." She turned to Raquella with an exaggerated grin that told Longarm she'd already pretty much guessed what had gone on between the young Mrs. Mayfair and the federal badge toter while Mr. Mayfair was laid up with a broken limb. "I do apologize for the trouble."

"It wasn't your fault, Deputy." Raquella's dark eyes coolly appraised Jessie sitting back in her chair with one boot hiked on her knee, shirt pulled back taut against her bosom, which, while not the size of Raquella's, was nothing to get her kicked out of bed for. "It is extraordinary, isn't it, for one so young and beautiful to be wearing a deputy sheriff's badge?"

"Believe me, ma'am," Jessie said with a single head wag, "it ain't by choice."

"I'm sure you do a wonderful job. You seem . . . very capable."

Longarm wasn't sure how she meant that, and Jessie didn't seem to, either, for she narrowed one eye at the Mexican woman, trying to study it out of Raquella's expression. Smiling brightly but somehow also tensely, Raquella turned to Longarm. "I thought we had parted ways, Marshal."

Longarm shook his head. "Change of plans. The man I'd come to pick up is currently . . . unavailable."

"I hope the situation isn't dire."

"We'll see."

Again, Longarm indicated the free chair at the table but hoping Raquella wouldn't take the offer. He sensed that it was apparent to Jessie that they'd slept together— if you could call it sleeping—and he sensed a building tension between the two women.

Raquella shook her head. "I do not want to interrupt your business discussion. I merely came downstairs for some brandy. The one that the doctor brought over is not to Malcolm's liking." She dipped her chin and added ironically, "Though he has nearly killed half of it already."

"Sure you won't sit down?" Jessie said. She cast a meaningful glance at Longarm. "I won't be here long. I got rounds to make. I'm just here for a nip or two."

It was Raquella's turn to glance at the rugged lawman. Then, her perfect cheeks flushing slightly, she dropped her eyes. "No, no. Like I said, I must fetch a bottle of brandy for my husband. It was nice meeting you, uh . . . Deputy Peckinpah."

"Call me Jessie," the deputy said coolly.

"Jessie, then," came the equally cool response. "And I am Raquella."

Jessie nodded at Raquella, who, in turn, nodded at Longarm, who just stood there with a big, stupid blush on his broad, saddle-leather face, gripping his chair back so hard with one hand he could vaguely hear it cracking.

He felt his hand slowly loosening its grip as Raquella turned and walked away, casting him one oblique glance over her shoulder before bellying up to the mahogany.

"So, Longarm," Jessie said as the lawman finally sat back down in his chair with a ragged sigh, "ain't you heard it's hard on a man's health to go around fuckin' married women?"

Longarm had just taken a sip of his second rye. It had barely hit his throat before it came back up, leaving his lips in a fine spray across the polished oak table. He looked at the tawny-haired deputy of Santiago, exasperated, then eased back in his chair, looking chagrined.

"It was that obvious?"

"Yep." Jessie threw back her third bourbon, stood, and doffed her hat. "Well, I reckon I'd best start makin' my rounds."

"Be careful out there."

"You're the one who better be careful," Jessie said, hitching her bone-handled Starr .44 up high on her left hip, then giving him a wink and tossing her head at the ceiling. "Up there."

The deputy sheriff of Santiago turned and sashayed away, chuckling.

* * *

After a slow, leisurely supper and another, postsupper rye, which he also took his time with, feeling the fatigue of his recent travails leeching slowly from his bones, Longarm lit a cheroot and took a slow turn around the town. The cantinas and saloons were doing a fairly brisk business for a weeknight, but Jessie seemed to have the vaqueros and gringo waddies on a short leash, everyone behaving themselves, including the dogs howling mournfully at the mariachi band tuning up in a smoky little watering hole on the far southern edge of the little border town.

He returned to the Red Ridge Inn just after sundown, intending to get a good long night's rest in a comfortable bed before riding south late the next day, on the trail of Wesley Wade. He passed the dining room, in which a good dozen or so stockmen were spinning the roulette wheel or bucking the tiger, with no sign of Buckshot Pete, who was apparently still sleeping off the previous night with the redheaded whore.

He rented a room from Señor Padilla, then hauled his gear up to the second floor. He was passing the Mayfairs' room, walking lightly so as not to disturb the couple—he really just felt like spending the rest of the night getting a good night's sleep without the complication of a married woman, however lovely—when their door latch clicked.

Longarm winced. He glanced over his right shoulder to see Raquella looking at him through the four-inch gap between the door and the frame. Her hair was down, and she wore a loose silk wrap. He could see the profile of nearly one entire breast shoved up close to the crack.

The breast rose and fell as she breathed. The tender nipple jutted. Her eyes were accusing.

"Home so early?" she said huskily.

Longarm kept his voice down. He could hear Mayfair snoring in the bed behind his wife. "Got a big day ahead."

"The deputy . . ." Raquella shook her hair back from her forehead. "She's beautiful."

"That she is."

"Well . . ." Raquella looked him up and down and gave a phony yawn, lightly slapping her hand over her mouth, her mostly naked breast still rising and falling slowly. "Good night, Marshal Long. Sleep well."

Longarm looked at the breast, recalled his and Raquella's frolic of the night before, and felt the old swelling in his loins. He chuckled, forcing himself to walk away from the Mayfairs' door.

"You, too, Mrs. Mayfair . . ."

He went into his own room and slept, but only after an hour of tossing and turning with the image of Raquella standing half-naked in her doorway blazed on the backs of his eyelids.

Women. They'd kill him yet.

He woke by habit at the first crack of dawn but forced himself to stay in bed until ten or so, smoking, drinking coffee, munching room service toast, and reading an old Phoenix newspaper he'd sent Padilla to fetch. After having the hotel proprietor haul up a tub and some scalding water, he lounged away another two hours in the hot suds before dressing in his more traditional attire—three-piece suit, including frock coat, vest, and whipcord trousers shoved down the tops of his mule-eared boots—heading out for a shave, a hair trim, and a leisurely lunch.

He saw neither hide nor hair of Buckshot Pete. He ran into Jessie in a little Mexican eatery near the sheriff's office, and she told him her pa had been up howling and carousing half the night, stumbling back to the Red Ridge Inn around five A.M., escorted by two whores this time, neither being the one of the previous night.

"If he doesn't get shot or drink himself to death," Jessie said over the smoking rim of a stone coffee mug, "he's liable to die screaming with the pony drip."

"It'd serve him right" was Longarm's opinion as he shoveled a forkful of eggs, beans, and roasted goat meat drenched in thick, spicy-sweet syrup into his mouth.

"You won't be the one doctorin' him."

"Get a whore to do it."

Jessie set her cup down. "How is Mrs. Mayfair this morning?"

"Holdin' her own, I reckon."

"Pretty woman."

"Funny," Longarm said, chewing another mouthful while the portly Mexican cook refilled his coffee mug, "she said the same thing about you."

"Oh?" Jessie cocked a brow. Her hazel eyes glowed especially bright in the light from the dusty little cantina's fly-specked front windows. "What do you think?"

"I think you're cute as a speckled pup, and you're gonna make some boy your own age happy as a coyote with a fresh bone one o' these days." Longarm stood, dropped some coins onto the rough wooden table, and picked up his scabbard and Winchester '73. "I'm off for Piñon Canyon. Keep that under your hat, will you? Lord willin' and the creeks don't rise, I'll see ya in a day or two."

He winked at the girl and headed off for the livery barn, where he'd already arranged for a good, broad-bottomed saddle horse to carry him off on the trail of Wesley Wade.

*   *   *

Two hours later, the sun was nearly down behind the western ridges, bringing out the soft reds and cool purples of early dusk.

Longarm put his rented speckle-gray gelding across a dry arroyo, through saguaros standing sentinel over a field of large, cracked, adobe-colored boulders, and out into an open stretch of the Sonoran Desert. There'd been no signs telling him so, but he figured he'd been on Chain Link graze for at least an hour, cutting across a corner of the Wade ranch on his way to Mexico.

He and the speckle-gray made their way through the last of the boulders, the horse's shod hooves clacking on stones and grinding the chipped caliche, a chaparral cock braying in the far distance. On the hot, dusty ride so far, Longarm had seen plenty of quail pecking around under mesquites, swinging their gaudy plumes around. But there were no mesquites here—just saguaros, barrel cactus, pipestem cactus, ocotillo, the dangerous cholla whose "leaping" thorns he was careful to swing the gelding wide of, and rocks.

Lots of rocks.

No wonder the ranchers down here needed so much land. Longarm hadn't seen enough grass out here to graze more than a single beef in virtually an entire square mile.

The horse tensed its back muscles and snorted.

Longarm reined it down between two saguaros and stared straight ahead. The horse snorted again, tossed its head contentiously.

Longarm's gut tightened as he narrowed his gaze, picking out three copper-skinned riders milling along the side of a knoll about a quarter mile ahead and to his right.

He couldn't see much from this distance, but he could see enough—the golden skin and leggings, the calico bandannas, the long black hair of the short, rangy riders, and their stocky pinto ponies—to conclude that they were Mescalero Apaches.

One of the three riders held his hand to his mouth. A few seconds later the chaparral cock crowed once more.

Only it was no chaparral cock, though the Mescalero gave a damn good imitation. One of the Indians threw an arm out toward Longarm as though to indicate him to other riders somewhere straight out ahead of them, probably holed up in the rocky hills on Longarm's left.

The lawman's heart quickened its beat as the three Apaches began kneeing their desert ponies down the knoll in his direction.

"Well, shit," he grumbled, slipping his Winchester '73 from the scabbard jutting up from beneath his right thigh. "Here, I was so damn sure I was gonna run into one of the Chain Link fellas, I'd plum forgot that 'Paches were still on the prod in this neck of Arizona."

He racked a shell into the Winchester's breech and looked around for cover. Picking out a low, steep-walled rocky ridge about a half mile beyond and on the left side of his trail, he decided to make for it. From there, he might be able to hold the Indians off.

Holding the Winchester in his right hand, he took the reins in his left, jerked his hat brim down low over his eyes so the wind wouldn't blow it off, and heeled the speckle-gray into an instant, lunging gallop. The horse was strong and fast and, more important, sure-footed. As they raced through the chaparral, the horse expertly

dodged cactus patches and boulders and did not hesitate
to leap the downed carcass of a bleached, long-dead
saguaro sprawled over two knee-high stones.

Longarm's gut rose into his throat as the horse landed
without the slightest slip or stumble beyond the fallen
saguaro, and he knew a moment of giddy excitement. If
he made it back to town, he'd commend the liveryman
on his selection of mounts. He'd needed a fast one that
knew the desert, and he'd gotten it.

Keeping his head low, Longarm glanced over his right
shoulder.

Rocks and cactus blocked his view of the Mescaleros,
but the crazed yips and howls were growing louder. Tan
dust lifted like smoke.

There was nothing quite like the horror of being chased
by Apaches. He'd been chased by these fierce Southwestern Indians before, and it was as keen a sensation—cold
and sharp and exhilarating all at the same time—as he'd
ever experienced. Part of the excitement came from the
nettling prospect of being staked out over a hill of fire ants
while the half-crazed desert warriors went to work on
your naked body with razor-edged knives and maybe
triggering a couple of arrows into your soft spots from
close range for added kicks and giggles.

Or, of course, there was always the trick of tying you
to a wagon wheel two feet above the ground and slow-
roasting you over a low fire after hacking away at your
nether regions . . .

Longarm looked ahead. In the corner of his left eye
he spied movement, and turned to see more copper-
skinned riders bounding over a low knoll from his left
flank, only about forty or fifty yards away. They dodged

and whipped expertly through and around the shrubs and boulders, their horses' unshod hooves clacking over the desert's carpeting of gravel and rocks.

They were so close that Longarm could see the lead rider, leaning low over his war-painted brown and white pinto, rack a shell into his Winchester carbine, and grin.

Chapter 10

Longarm ground his heels into the speckle-gray's flanks, urging even more speed as the Apaches howled like moon-crazed wolves on the blood scent.

The closest, grinning Mescalero had a good angle, and he was closing on the lawman fast from the direction of the gray's left hip. The warrior was so close now that Longarm could see he was tall for an Apache, and young. Probably fourteen or fifteen. His face was hideously painted, and as he drew within twenty feet of Longarm, he extended his Winchester carbine, which he'd likely stolen off the body of a dead soldier he'd slain with a bow and arrow, and angled the maw toward Longarm, straight out from his lunging pinto's right wither.

His coal black hair whipping in the wind behind him, the kid lifted the gun and grinned again as he narrowed an eye and stared down the Winchester's barrel.

Longarm snaked his own rifle across his belly, not aiming but bearing down on the kid with the instincts of a veteran lawman, and squeezed the trigger.

The Winchester roared, jerking against his belly.

Longarm kept both eyes on the trail ahead, but he heard the brave scream. The young warrior triggered his Winchester into the ground. In the periphery of the law-man's vision he watched the young warrior fly off his pinto's right hip and into the path of another warrior rid-ing hell-for-Indian-feathers about ten yards behind him.

There was a shrill horse scream along with the scream of another brave, and Longarm glanced over his shoulder to see the young brave's pinto veer off into the desert while the one behind him turned a savage somersault as it plowed into the brave whom Longarm had sent airborne. The second brave turned a similar somersault over his tumbling horse's head, and both braves and the horse were obscured in a churning dust cloud so that all Long-arm caught were fleeting glimpses of two jostling black heads, hooves, horses' tails, and flying rocks.

There were at least five more riders behind the tum-bling braves and the pinto, but they were too far away to worry about at the moment.

Longarm turned his head forward. The speckle-gray was galloping within fifty yards of the stony dike and closing fast. The horse didn't even seem to be tiring, just kept lunging forward and sending doggets of sand and prickly pear cactus flying up and behind it.

The first group of Apaches was still angling toward Longarm from the speckle-gray's left hip, but they were a good fifty yards away and having trouble closing the gap between them and the gray, as the desert in that di-rection was rockier and more boulder strewn. Longarm saw a notch in the low ridge growing larger before him. He angled the gray toward it.

As they reached the ridge's bottom, Longarm hauled

back on the horse's reins, then urged it more slowly up the boulder-strewn notch that angled steeply across the ridge's left side.

As the horse climbed, lunging off its rear hooves and grunting loudly, its bridle chains jangling, Longarm looked behind. The first group of Apaches was galloping through the boulders and saguaros behind him, spread out abreast and jerking around obstacles, their tan dust rising to be painted salmon by the setting sun.

Sensing an imminent end to their hunt, the Indians were screaming and whooping like banshees, a couple of the more eager warriors squeezing off shots with their cavalry-model Spencers and Trapdoor Springfields. A couple of the bullets plunked into the rocks three or four feet to either side of Longarm, threatening to pink him with a ricochet, but most were well wide.

As he and the gray neared the top of the dike, Longarm glanced back once more to see the first of the warriors galloping to within thirty yards of the dike's base.

"Come on, fella," Longarm urged, grinding his heels into the stalwart horse's flanks. "One more good push less'n you wanna be quartered by these bastards' squaws and served up for supper in the 'Pache wickiups tonight!"

As though in response to the lawman's warning, the gray gave a great *whoosh* of expelled air, and lunged up and over the crest of the dike.

"Ya made it, old son!" Longarm fairly yelled as he leaped out of the saddle, then slammed his Winchester's barrel against the sweaty mount's left hip, sending it trotting knock-kneed across the bluff's flat top.

The lawman sprinted to the edge of the dike and dropped to his hands and knees between two boulders, peering back down the steep notch that was still being swept by the gray's sifting dust. The first of the Indians had just reached the bottom of the dike. He was screeching at the top of his lungs as he batted his moccasins against his paint pony's dusty, sweat-silvered flanks.

As he started up the slope, nine others closed quickly, the first two of the nine checking their horses down to skidding halts.

Longarm quickly racked a fresh shell into his Winchester's chamber and drew a bead on the painted-faced warrior clattering up the slope with another whooping brave close behind him. Longarm triggered the Winchester and watched the first brave yelp and tumble straight back off his grulla's rump, throwing his Trapdoor Springfield up and behind him. If the second brave hadn't ducked, the rifle likely would have saved Longarm the trouble of having to shoot him.

As it was, the second brave merely snapped his head up toward the lawman, gritting his teeth and hardening his jaws. Dropping his rope reins across his still-climbing horse's neck, he jerked his Henry repeater toward Longarm and fired three quick shots, shooting and levering savagely.

The slugs slammed into the boulders on either side of the lawman, pricking his face with rock shards. A sliver lodged in his right eye, setting up a fierce stinging and causing that eye to water, tears dribbling down his dusty right cheek.

He bellowed a curse and fired toward the Apache with the Henry rifle, but the warrior had lunged on up the slope to his right and out of sight behind the boulder on that side of Longarm. Knowing the warrior would flank him soon, the fine hairs along his spine pricked with the notion that his goose was likely cooked.

He was outnumbered, shooting with only one eye, and the bastards were getting around him. So far, this had been one hell of a lousy trip out from Denver, and it didn't look to get much better . . .

Heart hammering, he fired two quick shots at the other howling warriors now beginning to storm up the slope behind the brave with the Henry. He winged one, who merely grunted as he kept his horse lunging on up the dike, and blew the left eye out of another before yet another yipping native fired three rounds from the lunging back of his Appaloosa, sending up more dust and rocks into Longarm's face and driving him back behind the lip of the dike's crest.

Longarm quickly thumbed fresh shells from his cartridge belt and into the Winchester. He racked one into the chamber, and, gritting his teeth from the sand and wafting dust and seeing nothing but a tan blur through his left eye, fired half-blindly at the trail to his right. He couldn't see the last three braves because of the backward curve of the dike's crest as well as the boulder he was hunkered behind, but he heard an enraged yelp followed a half second later by the thud of a body hitting the rocky trail, and the clatter of thrown gravel.

At least he'd gotten one more of the kill-crazy devils.

Downslope now, only dust.

On his right flank, hooves thundered as the warriors galloped up to the dike's crest and were working around behind him.

Longarm crabbed out from between the boulders as the first brave hammered toward him, triggering his Henry repeater, the bullets screaming over and around Longarm and one carving a hot line across the side of his right cheek. He triggered the Winchester twice, but the brave was pitching and dodging, and his right eye was stinging and watering, and both slugs sailed wide.

With a savage curse, he racked another fresh round into the breech. The futility of his situation badgered him. His legs turned to putty as four more of the howling, shooting braves galloped toward him, growing by leaps and bounds before him.

He was likely a goner, but he'd take one more of these kill-crazy devils with him . . .

A strange calm washed over him as he raised the Winchester to his cheek, squeezing his stinging eye closed, and fired. He took only mild comfort in seeing one more Apache turn a backward somersault off the rump of his galloping stallion. The others were coming fast and furious, bullets screeching around him and slamming into the rocks behind him, one ricochet kissing the lobe of his right ear.

The first Apache galloped straight toward Longarm, eyes wide with expectation as he jerked his smoking repeater to his cheek once more, drew a bead on the lawman's forehead. That unearthly calm continued to wash over the federal lawman, slowing time down, slowing the thudding horse hooves, the Indians' stygian hair whipping back behind them in the wind.

Longarm held his ground there on both knees. The howling brave with the Henry had him dead to rights—a strangely giddy feeling.

The brave grinned as he closed. Longarm saw the brave's tan index finger tighten over the Henry's trigger. Awaiting the bullet that would blow him into oblivion, Longarm automatically raised the Winchester.

He hadn't gotten it halfway to his shoulder before a round black hole appeared in the brave's right temple, just beneath his red calico bandanna. The brave flew back in his saddle, throwing his arms wide, his Henry flying out behind him. He tumbled off his mustang's right hip as the horse continued charging straight for Longarm, swinging right and away from him at the last second and throwing up dust and sand over Longarm's thighs.

Behind the horse, the head-shot Indian hit the ground, bounced, and rolled. One of the three other charging braves trampled the dusty, swarthy body as the mounted brave screamed suddenly, clutched his chest, and did an imitation of the preceding brave's death dive, leaving his horse riderless and swerving sharply away from Longarm and the lip of the ridge and heading out over the tableland.

A rifle barked shrilly.

Holding up his own Winchester, ready to continue firing, Longarm looked over his right shoulder. A hat poked above a boulder about thirty yards away. The figure held a Winchester in his gloved hands, and as Longarm watched, smoke and flames belched from the long gun's barrel.

Longarm turned forward to see another Apache flying off the back of his horse before smacking a boulder and whipping around in the air, then piling up on the ground in a twisted heap, blood from his broken head dripping down the side of the boulder above him.

The last of the Mescaleros who'd followed Longarm up the ridge checked his pinto down suddenly, holding his saddle-ring carbine in one hand while jerking back on his rope reins and looking around wildly, fear sparking in his chocolate eyes. Seeing that the brave was hesitating, Longarm rose to his feet and fired a shot on either side of the brave's prancing horse, blowing up dust and rocks.

The brave looked at Longarm, then reined his horse around sharply and, no longer whooping and yelling victoriously but casting wary looks over his shoulder, batted his moccasins against his mount's dusty flanks. Horse and rider galloped back the way they'd come, then turned sharply to drop back down the ridge and out of sight.

Automatically thumbing fresh rounds into his Winchester's loading gate, Longarm turned to the man just now rising from behind his covering boulder. "Thanks, partner," Longarm said, shaking his head with relief, "I owe you . . ."

He let his voice trail off when he saw that his savior wasn't some rifle-wielding prospector or a soldier separated from his cavalry patrol, but tawny-haired Jessie Peckinpah. She grinned snidely as she tramped toward the federal lawman, swinging her hips saucily and resting her smoking Winchester on her shoulder. Her wool shirt pulled back against her pert breasts, her deputy sheriff's badge bouncing about where her right nipple would be, Longarm couldn't help speculating in spite of his nearly being the guest of honor at a Mescalero torture party.

"What the hell are you doin' out here, young lady?"

"Got someone to watch the town for me, so I figured I'd ride out to back your play in Piñon Canyon."

She stopped near Longarm, poked her hat brim up her forehead, cocked one boot in front of the other, and proudly studied her handiwork sprawled before her and Longarm in the rocks and sage.

Longarm had moved forward, making sure the Indians were dead. He kicked the guns out of easy reach of even those who looked the deadest, and glanced over his shoulder at Jessie, her tawny hair blowing back from her smooth, dusty cheeks in the cooling evening breeze.

"Nice shootin'."

"Pa taught me back in his heyday." Jessie shook her head, sadly thoughtful.

When Longarm had kicked away the dead Indians' weapons, he leaped up onto a pile of boulders overlooking the lower country he'd ridden out of. Three mares' tails of dust dwindled into the distance across the salmon desert. The remaining Mescaleros had decided they'd live to fight another day.

Longarm leaped back down off the rocks and stood facing Jessie, who'd sat down on a flat-topped boulder to pluck cartridges from the shell belt encircling her slender waist and slip them through her Winchester's loading gate. "I do appreciate the help, Miss Jessie. Them Injuns were about to have me pincushioned to an old saguaro, but . . ."

"But what?" the girl said, cutting him off, her cheeks flushed and her eyes sharp with anger. "I'm no hothouse flower, Longarm. And I ain't wearin' this badge because I think it goes nice with this shirt."

She stood and walked toward him, staring up at him hard.

"I took over the job of lawdoggin' Santiago from Pa, knowin' full well it could get me killed. It's a responsibility I took upon myself, and I aim to do the job just like Pa or any other man would do it. Now, if Pa were back bein' himself, he'd likely have ridden out here to back you up at Piñon Canyon—wouldn't he? And you would have had no objection to that—would you? Probably would have even expected him to back you—wouldn't you?"

Longarm shrunk a little at the girl's anger as well as the logic of her argument.

"Well . . ."

"Of course you would. Since I'm fillin' in for him till he gets back on his feet again, it's my duty to back you up." Jessie shook her hair back from her hazel eyes and drew her shoulders back, thrusting her breasts out. "Now, we gonna stand around and palaver all night, or we gonna go fetch that federal prisoner of yours?"

Longarm dug in his shirt pocket for a fresh cheroot. "Just one question."

"What's that?"

"Who's watchin' over the town?"

"Pa himself."

Longarm was about to fire a match on his thumbnail, but he stopped and frowned down at the pretty young deputy sheriff of Santiago.

"He crawled down out of his digs at the Red Ridge Inn just as you were ridin' out of town," Jessie said, glancing toward where her horse grazed about a quarter mile off across the top of the mesa, not far from Longarm's. "His pride's achin'. He realizes how you've seen him, and what you know about him . . . him lettin' Wesley Wade go free. All that."

"So?"

"So, I think he's gonna make a try at pullin' himself together. He wanted to ride out after you, but he's in no shape for that. He's got the shakes so bad, he wouldn't have lasted a mile. If he don't keep drinkin' at least a little, he'll die. I told him if he wants to help he can watch over the jailhouse tonight, maybe try to keep the saloons quiet."

Jessie glanced back at Longarm, a vague beseeching

in her eyes. "He feels bad about who and what he's be-come, Longarm. Seein' you seein' him passed out with Miss Millie in his room yesterday . . . well, that's got to him bad. Might just be the hard knock he needs to get his brains shook back in place."

Longarm stared down at the girl. His heart ached for her. It was obvious how badly she wanted Buckshot Pete Peckinpah back in the saddle again. Unfortunately, Long-arm had seen too many men in Pete's current state never make it back. They'd die ugly in a smelly room some-where, alone or with a girl they'd paid to endure their last few hours, having been ostracized and all but forgotten by their friends and family.

"Yeah, maybe that's all he needs." Longarm tried to keep his skepticism out of his voice. He lit his cheroot and started tramping out toward where the speckle-gray grazed with Jessie's piebald. "Let's fetch ole Buckshot's prisoner back."

Chapter 11

Longarm and Jessie Peckinpah deadheaded for the lights of the roadhouse nestled in Piñon Canyon for nearly an hour before they finally rode into the yard of the place and checked their horses down.

The Pantera Cantina, nestled at the base of a high sandstone wall that blotted out the stars on this clear, cool desert night, was a sprawling, single-story adobe hovel with a brush roof and a broad fieldstone chimney from which the smell of piñon and mesquite smoke unraveled against the ridge's velvet backdrop. The cantina was fronted by a broad, stone-pillared gallery. Ollas hung beneath the gallery, and around these clay water pots shone pinpricks of orange light and occasional drifts of exhaled tobacco smoke.

Low voices, occasionally raised in laughter, rose from the men smoking there. High-crowned sombreros were silhouetted against the yellow-lit windows. Ambient light winked off the silver conchos decorating pistol belts and the ornate charro vests of the vaqueros or Mexican bandits who dwelled in this storied bordered region just east of Nogales.

"We might should've rode in from behind," Jessie said, keeping her voice low. Inside, someone was strumming a guitar. "That's Wade's big roan tied to the hitchrack yonder. He likely has men keeping watch out front."

Longarm looked toward the hitchrack to the right of the veranda's stone steps. The tall, long-legged roan stood with four others, head lowered, idly switching its tail. Four more horses stood at the hitchrack on the left side of the steps.

"I thought you said he usually rides out here with a small bunch."

"Them horses may not all be from the Chain Link remuda. There's lots of Mex cutthroats who hang out around here of a night as well. That don't mean we're any better off. Most of 'em can probably smell the law comin' from as far back as the San Pedro."

Longarm glanced at her. Jessie hiked a shoulder and said, "Want we should ride on around to the back, sneak up quiet like? If I remember right, there's a door back there."

"Nah. Unlike children, lawdogs are sometimes better off being both seen *and* heard." Longarm booted the speckle-gray forward and on into the yard, his hoof thuds rising sharply in the cool, quiet night, nearly drowning out the guitar strains emanating from inside the cantina. "Keep your long gun handy."

"You worry about your long gun, Longarm, and I'll worry about mine."

"Fair enough."

The lawman pulled his horse up to the far right end of the right hitchrack, and Jessie pulled in beside him. He looked over the other mounts. All, including Wade's big roan, were either Spanish barbs or Arabs, and they wore the Chain Link brand on their left withers. Longarm swung out of the leather, shucked his Winchester from his saddle boot, tossed his reins loosely over the hitchrack—he wanted to be able to grab them in a hurry—and stepped up onto the gallery.

The four men standing with their backs to the cantina's front wall either smoked or drank in silence, regarding him suspiciously. They were all dressed in Mexican garb—sombreros, short charro jackets, and deerskin leggings. One man wore a red sash around his waist. They all wore at least two pistols apiece. The man with the sash had a Sharps carbine leaning against the cantina wall behind him, between the batwing doors and a dust-streaked, lamp-lit window. The bone handle of a bowie knife jutted from the well of his high-topped, silver-tipped boots.

The man's thick handlebar mustache rose slightly as he lifted a quirley to his lips, and as he inhaled, causing the coal to glow, Longarm saw that he may have been dressed in Mexican garb, but his eyes were green and his hair was longish, wavy, and the gold of ripe wheat. He frowned warily at Longarm. His frown cut even deeper lines across his forehead when he saw Jessie walking up behind the federal lawman, and then he looked at the rifles both Longarm and Jessie were carrying up high across their chests.

Not giving the green-eyed gent time to ponder the cantina's visitors, Longarm blew past him and through the batwing doors, Jessie on his heels. Just inside the smoky room, Longarm stopped. Jessie pulled up off his right elbow, and they both cast their gazes quickly around the room occupied by only six other men, plus the apron, and a sporting girl.

The sporting girl was short, full-bodied, and obviously Mexican with her black eyes and hair. She had a wide, vixenish face, and she seemed to be having a great time straddling the lap of the handsome young dark-haired gringo in a pinto vest and funnel-brimmed Stetson seated at a table in the middle of the room. Two other men, both in ragged trail garb, sat around the handsome gent, one on his left, the other on his right, playing crib-bage with a bored air while flies buzzed around the two clear bottles on the table before them.

Two cigarettes sent smoke curling into the air above an ashtray cut from an airtight tin.

A little gray-haired Mex in a checked shirt and droop-ing mustaches sat on the stone steps at the back of the room, strumming a guitar and singing quietly in Spanish. A short black cheroot bobbed in the wizened right corner of his mouth. The head of a desert ram stared down from a post to his left.

Jessie said out of the side of her mouth, "Wade's the one with the *puta* on his lap."

"Stay here by the door."

Longarm strode forward past a couple of peons in dusty white pajamas and low-crowned sombreros who were rolling dice. No one paid any attention to him until he stood between Wesley Wade and the wall. The two men with Wade looked up from their cribbage game, frowning curiously at the tall gent with the Winchester standing over their boss with a grim look on his weath-ered, hard-eyed, mustached face.

The whore looked across the shoulder of Wade, who

sat with his back to Longarm, and ran her puzzled brown eyes up and down Longarm's frame. As she did, fear began to edge out the drunken celebration in those brown orbs, and her lower jaw slackened slightly.

Following the whore's glance, as well as that of his men, Wesley Wade jerked around in his chair. He had a weak-jawed, chinless, black-mustached face, with gray-blue eyes set below heavy black brows. His eyes owned the arrogance of the moneyed from birth. Likely, he'd never had to work for his luxuries, which included beautiful women. That and boredom and a general sense of entitlement had turned him cowardly mean, a cold-blooded killer.

"Hey," Wade said, incredulous, his own drink-shiny gaze running up and down Longarm as though at a bear who'd just wandered in out of the desert cold. "Who in the hell do you . . . ?"

At the back of the room, the guitar fell silent.

"Wesley Wade?" Longarm said.

"Who wants to know?"

"Federal law, you son of a bobcat bitch!"

Longarm rammed the butt of his Winchester straight forward against Wade's left temple. Wade grunted. The whore screamed. The man to Wade's right stumbled up out of his chair, dragging a big Dance and Brothers revolver out of his holster, hatchet face bunched with rage.

Longarm dropped the Winchester's barrel and squeezed the trigger. The explosion in the close confines rocked the room as the slug punched a neat round hole through the cutthroat's chest, sending him straight back over his chair while triggering his pistol into the floor.

He dropped the gun and piled up against the bar on

the far side of the room. From behind the bar, the sweating, bearded, cigar-chewing Mexican proprietor regarded Longarm with bald disdain.

Likely Wade and the other Chain Link riders were loyal customers.

As dirt slithered down from the rafters and the lanterns rocked, jostling shadows to and fro, the cutthroat to the left of Wade froze half out of his chair, staring wide eyed at the man Longarm had just beefed, his hand suspended over the pearl grips of the long-barreled .44 jutting up in the cross-draw position above his left hip.

Wade had grabbed his head and now he was sagging back and sideways in his chair, groaning, one arm looped around his chair back. The whore gave another shallow scream as the moneyed young killer continued to sag until he tipped over in his chair. The whore followed him to the floor, scrambling back away from him on her hands and knees and gritting her teeth at Longarm, eyes flashing like those of an angry puma.

"What you do that for, gringo *bastardo*? Wade is my"— she hesitated, looking for the right word in English— "boyfriend!"

"Party's over, princess."

Longarm loudly ejected the spent round from the Winchester's breech. The empty casing hit the stone floor with a *ping* as the lawman rammed a fresh cartridge into the rifle's breech, bearing down on the man who was still frozen half out of his chair and now looking at Longarm with pink-faced exasperation, his scarred lower lip quivering as though he'd caught a fierce chill.

Longarm narrowed an eye at him. "Pull your hand away from that hogleg and reach for the ceiling. Go ahead and tickle it with your fingertips."

As the gent did as he was told, straightening his back and slowly raising both hands, Longarm glanced quickly toward the front of the room. He'd heard boots scuffing and spurs ringing as the men from the gallery had scrambled in to see what the shooting was about, but Jessie had loudly racked her Winchester, getting their attention. She had all four men with their backs against the wall, hands raised to their shoulders.

"Get 'em up there!" ordered the deputy sheriff of Santiago, waving her Winchester at the tallest man scowling down at her, the yellow-haired rider with a quirley smoldering between his long pink lips.

They were all jerking puzzled, anxious glances toward Longarm.

"Jesus Christ!" carped Wesley Wade, rolling onto his side while clutching his bloody left temple with his left hand.

He glanced up at Longarm, blinking blood out of his left eye. Both eyes looked rheumy as they rolled around in their sockets. Wade was exasperated, but in his current condition there wasn't much he could do about it. Longarm reached down and pulled the pearl-gripped .44 from the cross-draw holster on Wade's left hip. He looked around the kid's rangy person but saw no signs of a hideout or a knife.

"Just how bad you wanna die, lawdog?" bellowed the yellow-haired, green-eyed gent with the quirley in his teeth.

Longarm let his glance pass over the man as he turned to Jessie. "Get their gun belts, Deputy. Have 'em take off their boots and tip 'em upside down."

Jessie said, "You heard the man, boys. I hope you done washed your feet in the last few days."

Longarm waved his Winchester at the man standing before him. "You, too. Out of your boots. First, toss over that shell belt."

"What?"

Longarm narrowed his eye again as he stared down his Winchester's barrel, planting a bead on the man's broad, sun-burned forehead. The man's face slackened slightly. When he'd removed his pistol belt and tossed it to Longarm, he stepped back and used his right boot to kick out of his left.

The whore was still kneeling beside Wade, looking around at the room as though she'd suddenly awakened to find herself somewhere she hadn't expected, her broad but clean-lined cheeks flushed with fear, anger, and disbelief.

"Miss," Longarm said, "I don't reckon you're sportin' a shootin' iron, since I'd likely see one through that sheer little setup. Am I right?"

She scowled up at him, throwing her arms out as if to give him a better look. The dress she wore was green silk, and there was barely enough of it to ram down a pistol barrel. One strap had dropped down her arm, exposing nearly all of her left breast, including half a nipple. She seemed in no hurry to cover herself.

"Pull Wade's boots off," Longarm ordered the whore.

"Pull 'em off yourself!"

Longarm was above laying out an unarmed woman with his Winchester's butt, but she didn't know that. He stared at her hard and made a muscle in his cheek twitch. She recoiled a little, buying the bluff.

"All right, all right—a big, angry gringo *bastardo*, huh?"

"Somethin' like that."

As Wade moaned and clutched his bleeding temple, the whore grabbed one of his hand-tooled, ornately stitched calfskin boots and bit her lip as she pulled. When the boot came off, a pearl-handled, brass-hilted knife of shiny tempered steel dropped out, encased in a light, black leather sheath. Longarm gave the knife a kick, sending it sliding between the feet of the scar-lipped man, who had one boot off and was hopping around as he pulled off the other.

The knife hit the base of the bar with a thud. The scar-lipped man looked at it, looked at Longarm, snarled, then pulled his second boot off with a chuff of expelled air. As the whore pulled off Wade's second boot with nothing else coming out of it, Longarm looked toward the front of the room.

Jessie was aiming her Winchester at the four other cutthroats, all in various stages of disarming themselves and removing their boots. The night air sifting over and around them carried the sour odor of sweaty socks and unwashed feet into the saloon's depths.

Jessie looked at Longarm and pinched her nose. "Is this really necessary?"

"I'm havin' second thoughts my own self," Longarm quipped. "Take their guns."

"You got no right to take our guns," objected the yellow-haired, green-eyed man as he kicked a black boot against the cold woodstove standing between him and the bar. "What if we run into 'Paches on our way back to the Chain Link? There's been Mescaleros about."

"Ran into a few ourselves," Longarm said. "I suggest you ride hard and fast . . . once you catch your horses."

The yellow-haired man's green eyes snapped wider

and fired invisible daggers across the room at Longarm. "What the hell you mean by that? You ain't gonna take *our horses, too*?"

Longarm shoved Wesley Wade belly down on the floor and planted a knee against the killer's back. He leaned his rifle against a ceiling joist, within easy reach, and pulled a pair of handcuffs from his cartridge belt. "Nah, that'd slow us down. But we're gonna scatter 'em to the four winds. Keep you boys off our trail as long as possible."

"You're in so much shit, lawdog," Wade grumbled, cheek against the stone floor as Longarm drew the young killer's arms behind his back, crossing his wrists. "When my pa gets wind of this, he's gonna burn you down hard! *Ouch—goddamnit, that's too tight!* When he finds out what you done here, your folks back home ain't never gonna recognize you . . ."

Longarm jerked Wade to his unsteady feet and grabbed his Winchester. At the front of the cantina, Jessie had four shell belts looped over both of her arms, and the four Chain Link cutthroats were once again standing with their backs against the wall, hands held high above their heads. All were in their stocking feet, boots scattered before them.

They were shuttling glares between her and Longarm, who, keeping his rifle aimed in the general direction of the whore and the scar-lipped Chain Link rider, shoved Wesley Wade toward the front of the room. He had the scar-lipped rider's pistol belt slung over his left shoulder. As he walked up to the yellow-haired man standing against the wall, he said, "If I see any of you in the doorway before Deputy Peckinpah, myself, and this ringtail sonofabitch you call a boss is out of sight, I'll be force-feedin' you a forty-four caliber blue whistler."

The yellow-haired gent stared hard at Longarm, so enraged that his right eye twitched slightly and sweat oozed from the large pores on his fleshy, sun-blistered face. "Boy, oh, boy. Amigo, you enjoy the time you have left. Killin' you ain't gonna be hard, and when you go down, you're goin' down howlin'."

Longarm stopped and grinned at the man, who was as tall as Longarm himself. The man grinned back, tightly.

"What's your name, friend?" Longarm asked.

"Savage. Lou Savage. I'm Mr. Wade's *segundo*."

"I wouldn't expect the second-in-command to be out here so late at night."

Savage hiked a shoulder. "What's it to you? Mr. Wade knows Wesley'll ride out here no matter what, so he sends me now to keep an eye on things."

"You're doin' a good job, Mr. Savage."

"Fuck you."

Longarm jerked his rifle down and buried the butt in Savage's solar plexus. Savage jerked forward with a chuff of expelled air, clutching both arms across his belly and dropping to his knees with a dull thud against the flagstones.

"Why . . . you . . . sonofabitch . . . !"

"Stay away from town, Savage." Longarm shoved Wesley Wade on out the door and onto the gallery. "I see you or the head honcho or Arroyo Simms or any of these other polecats in Santiago as long as I'm there, I'll arrest you on the spot for vagrancy."

He glanced at Jessie. "Wait here a minute, Deputy."

Jessie kept her rifle leveled on the men with their backs to the wall. "Whatever you say, Marshal."

Longarm went outside, shoved Wade off the veranda and into the yard, where the addlepated young killer dropped to his knees in the dirt. Quickly, Longarm untied all the horses except for Wade's roan, and, with three quick shots in the air, sent them galloping hell-for-leather into the night. Just as quickly, he prodded Wade into his saddle, then backed the roan, his own speckle-gray, and Jessie's pie away from the hitchrack and into the yard.

Swinging up into the saddle, he swung around and aimed his Winchester at the cantina's lantern-lit doorway. "Come on, Deputy—we're burnin' moonlight!"

Jessie pushed through the batwings and clomped across the veranda. While Longarm kept his rifle aimed at the doorway and the men standing stiffly inside, swinging their heads to peer over the batwings, Jessie swung up into the leather.

"All set." Breathing hard, she smiled at Longarm. "Let's get Pa's prisoner back to Santiago."

"Good idea."

Longarm swung the speckle-gray around and, tugging hard on the big roan's reins, headed off across the cantina's yard, past the well and corrals and into the dark, star-canopied desert beyond.

Chapter 12

"You hit me too hard, lawdog," Wesley Wade complained as Longarm reined his speckle-gray to a halt in a copse of moonlit willows and gnarled mesquite. "I mean, if you wouldn'ta hit me so damn hard, scrambled my brains for me, I mighta considered goin' light on ya."

Sitting the big roan slump-shouldered and hatless behind Longarm, Wade shook his head. "But now . . . hell, when the boys from the Chain Link come to bust me out, you're gonna take a good, long time, dyin' . . ."

Longarm swung down from the speckle-gray's saddle and tramped back to Wade's horse. A few miles from the cantina, he'd stopped and tied the young killer's cuffed wrists to his saddle horn, so he couldn't tumble out of the saddle and try to escape across the moonlit desert. Now Longarm pulled his barlow knife from a pocket of his frock coat, reached up, and cut the rope free of the apple.

"You hear me, lawdog?" Wade's voice was weak, pain-racked, but edged with exasperation.

Obviously, the kid wasn't accustomed to being treated so shabbily. Jessie had told Longarm that the young killer had grown up in a sprawling Spanish-style casa at the Chain Link and was educated for a few years in Eastern boarding schools before being kicked out and sent back to Arizona, where he'd been a blight on the country around Santiago ever since. Both parents were hard people, and while it was believed they'd tried to raise him right, they'd given up on him while remaining inexplicably protective.

Probably didn't want to believe they'd raised a worthless scoundrel, Longarm thought as he closed his knife and dropped it back down in his pocket.

"Hey." Wade prodded Longarm with his stocking foot. "I'm talkin' to you."

"I thought it was you," Longarm drawled, pulling the kid out of the saddle none too gently, then, grabbing his coiled rope, shoving Wade off toward a mesquite, the leaves of which dripped with silver moonlight. "Flies don't buzz that loud."

"You rankle me, lawdog. That's what I'm sayin'."

When Longarm had pushed Wade down against the tree, the young killer looked up at him, the moonlight showing the bloody, dark bruise on his left temple. "But it ain't too late. If you let me go right now, send me back to the Chain Link on my hoss, I'll tell my pa, Savage, and Arroyo Simms to go easy on ya. In spite of how you so badly mistreated Savage, too. That there was an even bigger mistake. Why, Lou—he's—"

Longarm cut the killer's sentence off by slipping his red neckerchief up across his mouth, drawing it tight behind his head, and double-knotting it. The kid squirmed and grunted behind the cloth, gagging slightly.

"Thank you," Jessie said, coming up behind Longarm. "And they say girls do nothin' but yap."

Longarm used his rope to tie Wade snug against the mesquite, so he wouldn't have to keep such a close watch on the kid.

"Figured we stop here, rest the horses, and fill our canteens." Longarm rose, ignoring the muffled complaints and insults emanating from behind Wade's neckerchief. "Maybe catch a few winks ourselves. It's been a long night, and we'll want to be sharp once the sun rises."

Jessie glanced to the east, where false dawn glowed dully, silhouetting the toothy ridges of the desert mountains. "Be light in an hour or so." She lightly kicked Wade's left foot. "You think his boys followed us?"

"Not that I could tell. But they know where we're headed. Likely, they'll go back to the Chain Link, round up some more men, including the kid's old man, and meet us in town sometime tomorrow."

Longarm unsaddled his horse, slinging his gear across a deadfall cottonwood. When he'd done the same to the roan, he tied both horses near the creek and some tall grama grass, then grabbed his canteen and walked off toward a bend in the stream, down from the horses. Jessie had tended her own mount, and now she followed him. When he knelt beside the stream, he saw her do likewise a few feet upstream from him.

Longarm doffed his hat and ducked his head in the cool, refreshing water, coming up blowing luxuriously, enjoying the feel of the fluid streaming under his shirt collar and down his hot, sweaty chest. The night was cool, but it had been a long, hot ride.

He ducked his head again, drank deeply.

When he lifted his head out of the water, he saw a

shadow slide across the bank to his right. He turned his head sharply, reaching for the Colt on his left hip, water streaming down his face.

He stayed his hand on the .44-40's grips, leaving the piece in its holster. Jessie stood before him. She held her rifle across her chest, sort of wringing the long gun in her hands.

The young law bringer shook her head slowly. Her voice was rich and deep, just loud enough for Longarm to hear above the gurgling stream. "You walked in there like you wasn't afraid of nothin'."

Longarm cleared his throat, swept a fist across his nose. "What's that, Miss Jess—?"

"I never seen anything like that, Custis. Those cutthroats feared you." She licked her lips. "I ain't so sure I wasn't afraid myself of what you'd do . . ."

She continued to squeeze the rifle in her hands. She stared at him, but because the moon was behind her, he couldn't see her eyes. Her hair hung down across her shoulders, framing her face. Her chest rose and fell slowly, evenly, heavily, the wanton orbs drawing the wool shirt taut with each inhalation.

Longarm could fairly smell the want on the girl. The urgent need. It was as affecting as a potent shot of twice-distilled busthead.

Suddenly, she let her rifle drop in the grass and immediately began unbuttoning her shirt. Longarm's heart turned a flip-flop in his chest, and his loins pricked with a desire every bit as hot and demanding as the girl's.

He kicked out of his boots and began unbuttoning his shirt, watching Jessie fling her own shirt away and lift her camisole up and over her head.

Moonlight limned her pale, firm, pink-tipped orbs. It

illuminated the stray wisps of hair that slithered across each breast as she unhitched her cartridge belt and let her holster and gun drop into the grass at her feet. She stepped back and, holding Longarm's smoldering, lust-crazed gaze with her own, kicked out of her boots, then leaned forward, breasts sloping toward the ground, and shoved her faded denims down her legs, wiggling her hips deliciously.

She pulled her white panties down with her jeans, and the moonlight bathed her pale, well-turned legs.

No sooner had the deputy sheriff of Santiago shucked out of her clothes than Longarm had kicked out of his own. He doffed his hat and, iron-hard shaft jutting and bobbing before him, stepped toward her and grabbed her shoulders.

He drew her against him, feeling her breasts flatten against his belly, and kissed her hard.

Her mouth opened for him, and she pressed her tongue against his, nibbled his lips and mustache and sucked at his teeth. She stepped into him, hooking one of her legs around one of his, pressing her silky mound against his left thigh, rising up onto her toes to run the hot fur across his balls and upthrust member, rubbing harder and harder until he could feel her nether lips open, became aware of a syrupy wetness against his leg.

She moaned as he kissed her, reached down and grabbed his cock in both her hands, stroking him until he felt as though his head had been cleaved with an ax. She pulled away with another groan, glanced down, and exclaimed softly but raspily, "God, Custis—you're *huge!*"

She sank down before him, looking up at him with grave desperation as she stroked his throbbing, purple-headed shaft with her cheek. Holding him with one hand, she slathered him with her tongue—from his balls to the tip of his cock—until he was groaning and sighing and feeling as though his heart had been wrenched in two.

He'd assumed from what she'd told him before that her virtue, as they say, might have been uncompromised. Silly him. This girl had obviously taken a tumble or two before, had learned without inhibition how to set a man's soul on fire and blow his proverbial boots off in the process.

When she had him dripping wet with her own saliva and shuddering like a nervous dog in a thunderstorm, she released him, licking her lips, then turned over onto her hands and knees. Glancing over her right shoulder, she waggled her tight, round ass in the moonlight, then dropped her head down between her shoulders, hair brushing the ground, moaning.

Longarm dropped to his knees, crouched over the girl, grabbed her sloping breasts in his hands. Her nipples were rigid against his palms. He pulled her gently back toward him until her sopping snatch touched the mushroom head of his swollen shaft. Feeling her portal open wider, hearing her groan deep in her throat, seeing her lift her face toward the stars so her thick hair tumbled down her back, he slid all the way inside her.

"Oh," she said. "Oh . . . oh . . . oh . . . *God* . . . !"

Longarm hammered against her, squeezing her tits, which leaped like wild little animals in his hands, pulling her back against him, then pushing her away, in and out, in and out, until they both reached the apex of their bliss.

He held her against him as their spasms dwindled. She

was so spent that she sagged, a deadweight, in his hands. When he finally finished firing his jism inside her, he eased her gently onto the grass and sagged, exhausted and sweating, down on top of her back, breathing so hard that he puffed her hair out away from her neck.

"Hey!" It was Wesley Wade yelling from the other side of the trees, out of sight beyond some boulders. He'd worked his gag out of his mouth. "What the hell you two doin' over there? You ain't fuckin' like a coupla minks on Uncle Sam's time, are ya?"

When Longarm and Jessie had snuggled awhile, leaving Wade to his own devices, they each wearily climbed back into their clothes and pistol belts. Jessie picked up her rifle and dusted it off. She looked at Longarm.

"Now I know what Mrs. Mayfair found so enchanting about you."

"Yeah, I been told I have a right fetching smile."

"That ain't all you got." Jessie shook her hair out of her eyes. "A man like you could ruin a girl for the other boys around town."

"A girl like you could do the same to a gent like me." Longarm pulled the deputy sheriff of Santiago to him, crushing her breasts against his chest, and kissed her.

"You don't mean it," she said when he let her go.

"I do mean it. But I hope you won't go thinkin' there's anything more here than . . ."

"Oh, hell—I wasn't born yesterday!"

The girl chuffed, disgusted, and stomped back toward their makeshift camp. Longarm chuckled as he dropped to his knees and dunked his head in the stream once more, drinking deeply. When he'd had his fill, he picked up his canteen, donned his hat, and headed back to where Jessie was busy saddling her horse.

Wade, whose wet neckerchief hung twisted and slack beneath his chin, looked at Longarm suspiciously. "What were you two doin' back there?"

"Fuckin' like minks," Longarm said, grabbing his own saddle blanket.

Jessie kept her back to him but she glanced over her shoulder. A devilish smile caused her eyes to glitter before she turned her head quickly back to her piebald.

Wade slid his uncertain gaze between them. "Pshaw! You was not. A girl like Jessie Peckinpah wouldn't look twice at a big, mean scoundrel like yourself." Wade kicked dirt with his stocking foot. "Would you, Jessie? A girl like you prefers the wild ones with money . . . like myself."

"There you got it, Wesley," Jessie said, reaching under the pie to fasten the latigo. "I'm gonna have just an awful time while you're in the lockup, keepin' my hands off'n a spineless, weak-chinned, rabbit-eyed, bush-whackin' rake like you."

"Careful there, Deputy," Wade growled. "I was sorta thinkin' of goin' easy on you when the boys from the Chain Link ride in and spring me. The marshal here's gonna die painful and bloody. Don't make me reconsider about you."

"Shut up, Wade," Longarm said, tightening his own latigo cinch. "Or you'll ride with that gag so far down your throat it'll give you indigestion."

He glanced at Jessie. She'd saddled and bridled her mount and was staring back in the direction from which they'd come. Her eyes were pensive, wary.

Wade saw the look, too. "Yeah, you best be scared,

Deputy Peckinpah. 'Cause when the boys catch up to you—"

Longarm shot the killer a warning look. Wade closed his mouth but stared at Longarm, smiling.

Chapter 13

Several miles from Santiago, Longarm led his prisoner
and young Deputy Sheriff Peckinpah off the main trail
that they'd picked up after crossing the border. They
threaded their way cross-country through the chaparral,
approaching Santiago from a dry wash, then weaving
between shacks and clomping through an alley until the
main drag lazed before them, quiet in the blazing mid-
morning, midsummer sun.

Almost no one was out. A few horses slumped in the
shade of a couple of different brush arbors fronting business establishments to Longarm's right and on the other
side of the rutted, chalky street.

"All clear," the dusty, sweaty lawman croaked.

"I wouldn't expect for any Chain Link men to be in
town yet. It's a long ride from the headquarters."

"Better safe than sorry."

Longarm urged the speckle-gray out into the main
street, turning left and jerking Wesley Wade's big roan
along behind him, Jessie riding drag and holding her rifle

across her saddlebows. Wade rode slouched in his saddle. Not only was he still addled from Longarm's clubbing but his hooch had long since worn off, and he was likely feeling the agonizing affects of a hangover in the ninety-degree heat.

Longarm reined in when he saw a bedraggled-looking character standing under the awning of a drugstore, flies buzzing around his head. The man was pot-bellied, wearing a grimy long-sleeved undershirt with suspenders holding up his patched and threadbare moleskin trousers. He held a double-barreled 10-gauge shotgun in one hand; a sheriff's badge hung slack on his shirt.

Buckshot Pete Peckinpah smiled sheepishly out from beneath the brim of his battered Stetson.

"Brought my dog back, did ya? I been lonesome for him."

Longarm regarded his old friend grimly. "Think you can hold on to him this time?"

Buckshot Pete sleeved a lock of gray-brown hair away from his right eye and regarded Longarm seriously, with more than a tad of beseeching. "Yeah, I think I can."

"You look like shit."

"Don't feel half that good."

Jessie rode up beside Longarm and regarded her father with an expression similar to the federal badge toter's. "You best go to bed, Pa. I'll take over now."

"You've taken over long enough, Jessie. It's time I did my own job."

Longarm booted the speckle-gray ahead slowly. "Do as she says, Pete. Me and Wesley won't be here long, anyways. I intend to change horses fast as I can, down a quick meal, fill my canteens, and head for the railroad line up north. Wanna be well outta here before them diamond-backs from the Chain Link show up."

Buckshot Pete was walking along under the brush arbors, keeping pace with Longarm, his daughter, and Wesley Wade's hang-headed roan. He shook his head. "I wouldn't do that, Custis. Injuns on the prod out there. Got word that two ranches were burned yesterday and early this mornin'. Them Mescaleros'll be watchin' any trails with water on 'em, and there ain't but two trails, water or no water, through the mountains between here and the railroad."

Longarm reined up again. "Shit."

Buckshot Pete stopped. He leaned weakly forward to rest an arm on an awning support post. The sun found his face and glistened on the sweat dribbling down his pasty, patch-bearded cheeks. "It's a passel of warriors up from Mexico. They'll likely have their fun for a week or two, then light a shuck back to the Sierra Madres."

"In the meantime," Longarm said, casting a dark glance in the direction of the Chain Link headquarters, "this kid's old man's gonna show up with a small army of his cutthroats, makin' things a might prickly around here. I'd rather take my chances in the open country."

Buckshot Pete shook his head. "You won't make it, Custis. My last deputy—I mean, the one before Jessie—died out there when the Mescaleros wearied of rez life just like they're doin' now. Sent him back to town in a clay pot tied to a burro's back."

Longarm winced.

"Besides, there's a contingent of soldiers out of Fort Huachuca that runs through here once a month. The captain's a madman for promptness, never been so much as a day late in the past year and a half. He's due in three days."

"So," Longarm said, thinking on it, "this being Tuesday, he'll likely be here on Friday?"

"I expect him Friday before noon."

Longarm glanced at Jessie before returning his skeptical gaze to her father. "Can we hold out that long—just the three of us?"

Wesley Wade said, "Damn, Sheriff—you look like you could use a drink. If this federal scalawag would cut my hands loose, I'd toss you a dime for a shot of red eye." He wrinkled a mock curious brow. "Or you still drinking mescal these days?"

Buckshot Pete looked at the flat-eyed young killer, threw his shoulders back, and lifted his chin, pale cheeks finally showing some color.

Longarm booted his speckle-gray forward and tugged at the killer's lead lines, heading off down the street once more. "We'd best get this jasper behind lock and key before somethin' bad happens and we cheat the hangman out of his pay."

When Longarm and Jessie had pulled up to the hitchrack fronting the jailhouse, and Buckshot Pete was catching up at a fast hop-skip that seemed to detonate a small blast inside his head with every step, Longarm swung down from the speckle-gray and reached up to cut Wesley's cuffed wrists free of his saddle horn.

"Oh, lordy, that was a long, miserable ride," the young killer said, swaying back against the side of his horse. "I sure could use a shot of somethin'—"

Longarm saw the kid glance over his left shoulder and down toward Longarm's holstered .44. A half second later the killer was swinging both cuffed fists around and up on an interception course with Longarm's chin.

He didn't get his fists even half-raised before Longarm rammed the butt of his Winchester solidly against the killer's already bruised and swollen left temple. "Uhnnn," Wade said, falling against the big roan, his eyes rolling back in their sockets.

The roan whinnied and sidestepped, and the kid plopped straight back on his ass in the street, dust wafting up around him. He sat there, dusty hair in his eyes, looking stunned.

"You'd think he'd learn," Jessie said from the jailhouse veranda.

"Go ahead and give him another one o' them, Custis," Buckshot Pete said, gritting his teeth as he stared down at Wade from beside his daughter. "Save us a whole lotta trouble in the long run."

"I know the hangman in Denver," Longarm said, grabbing the collar of Wade's shirt and jerking the mon-eyed outlaw to his feet. "He gets paid ten dollars for every hanging. I know 'cause we play friendly poker in the Black Cat from time to time." He gave the still stunned Wade a stiff kick in the ass, propelling the young outlaw up the porch steps between Jessie and Buckshot Pete. "If he'd heard I'd cheated him out of two silver cartwheels, he'd be sore as hell."

"Imagine," Buckshot Pete said, throwing open the jailhouse door ahead of Longarm and Wade. "Ten dollars just to hang a man. Hell, I'm in the wrong line of work."

Longarm prodded the ragged-heeled, shamble-footed Wade through the door and kept prodding the young killer until Longarm had him in a middle cell and Buckshot Pete was closing the barred door on him and turning the key in the rusty lock. Wade glared through the bars at Longarm, blood dribbling down from the growing purple goose egg on his temple. He hardened his jaws, but his eyes were pain-racked, out of focus.

"There's another reason you're gonna die hard, you son of a bitch. Just wait till Pa and Lou Savage get here. Just you wait!"

He squeezed the bars in his hands as he continued glaring at the federal lawman, then, stretching his lips back from his teeth as another pain bolt lanced his noggin, staggered over to the cell's lone cot and dropped belly down on top of it. He laced his hands behind his head, groaning facedown in his pillow, shoulders rising and falling sharply.

Longarm turned to Buckshot Pete, who was returning his key ring to a drawer of the desk in the room's rear corner, under a snarling bear's head mounted above a chained gun rack on one wall, a map of San Isabel County on the other. "Who is this Savage fella, Pete?"

"A hired gun from Nacogdoches. If you ain't heard his name, you must recollect seein' his dog-faced countenance on a wanted dodger—only of course them pencil sketches don't bring out the green in his evil eyes."

Longarm hiked a hip on a corner of the sheriff's desk, a pensive expression on his face. "There's gettin' to be too many lobos for this old sheepherder to keep track of. You're right about them eyes. I doubt I'll forget him now that I've seen him. Him and Arroyo Simms make quite a pair."

"Been introduced to Simms, have you?"

"Years ago. I thought he was dead."

"Lots of dead men find second lives down here."

Jessie stood at the open door, staring into the sunlit street, holding her rifle across her thighs. She glanced over her shoulder. "I'll tend our mounts and keep an eye on things out here while you boys palaver."

She studied her father worriedly for a moment, then slid her slightly oblique, conspiratorial gaze to Longarm before moving on out the door and pulling it closed behind her.

Buckshot looked at the door then sagged down in the squawky swivel chair behind his desk. "Ain't she somethin'?"

"She's a little more than somethin'." Longarm felt the tips of his ears warm as he remembered taking the man's polecat of a ring-tailed daughter last night in the moonlit mesquites. "Who's her mother? I don't recollect you bein' married, Pete."

"Never was. Me and Eileen got together up in Colorado— little town of Creede way up high in the San Juans. Sharp-toothed little mining berg. I was called in to pull its teeth or at least file 'em down a little. Eileen ran a saloon."

Yawning wide, Pete leaned forward and ran both his hands down his face and through his shaggy, graying hair.

"When I left, I didn't know I'd left something behind . . . until three years ago, when Eileen wrote and said she was dyin' of a cancer in her throat and would I take our daughter? Eileen was worried that Jessie on her own might take the wrong fork in the trail and, while I probably wouldn't offer much in the way of guidance for a young girl of fifteen, I was all the hope she had."

"Surprisingly, you've done well, you old reprobate," Longarm said, slinging his hat against Pete's shoulder with begrudging affection.

"Unfortunately, she's about all the good I've done here."

"That ain't what Jessie told me. She said you turned Santiago civilized. It's only in the past few months you fell into the trough filled with busthead. Tell me, Pete— she couldn't have been that damn unexpendable."

"Oh, Custis." Buckshot Pete sagged back in his chair but raised his dirty hands to trace a bodacious figure in the air before him. "That girl had the finest curves I've seen. Of course, she was a rascal, but then I never been much of a judge of women."

He let his hands fall back into his lap and fidgeted around in his chair, making it squawk. "When she told me two days before we was to walk down the aisle she was takin' off with a gambler from Abilene . . . I don't know. I just felt like a boulder done flattened me. I'd been alone so long, with only whores to warm my feet and haul my ashes. And, shit, I ain't gettin' any younger. I ain't afraid of many things, Custis—you know that. But one thing I am afraid of is growin' old alone. Of dyin' alone."

Buckshot opened the drawer in which he'd dropped the keys and stared hard at the corked brown bottle standing there up against the door's front panel. "Seemed I just wanted my fear numbed, not to mention the embarrassment of ole Buckshot Pete gettin' left at the altar, made a damn laughingstock of the whole county."

He held out a pale, veined hand before him. It shook. He grabbed it with the other one but they were both shaking as he held them against his paunch.

Longarm bit back his emotion. He knew some of what Pete was going through. He, too, harbored similar fears, but he'd managed to dilute them in work. "Go on, Pete," he said softly. "You'd better take a drink."

"Nah, shit, I'm quittin'. I done made a fool o' myself for the last time."

"You can't go cold turkey. As bad as you are, you'll die."

"I got some beer." Buckshot Pete rose from his creaky chair and ambled over to the far side of the room, where Longarm now saw there was a trapdoor embedded in the floor, a dusty metal loop ring showing. "It stays good and cool here in the cellar. I know you're a rye man, but you want one o' these?"

"Why not?"

Buckshot had just grabbed the door's ring and begun to pull when the jailhouse's front door opened suddenly. Jessie poked her head in.

"Custis! Pa! You both better git out here. We got company."

Buckshot Pete let the trapdoor drop with a raspy thump, dust wafting up around his knees. As he tramped back to the desk for his shotgun, Longarm grabbed his rifle and took long strides to the front door, which Jessie had left yawning wide and through which he could hear the galloping thuds of a dozen approaching riders.

Chapter 14

Longarm stepped onto the jailhouse veranda and peered eastward along the main street. A dozen or so riders were galloping toward the jailhouse with a hard-jawed old gent in a buckskin vest and white, black-banded Stetson riding point. The others were flanked out around him on their dusty, sweat-lathered ranch ponies.

"They made better time than I figured they would," Jessie said darkly, standing at the edge of the veranda to Longarm's right.

Longarm moved left along the porch, putting as much space between him and the girl as possible. Buckshot Pete tromped out through the open door to stand between them, about five feet from each of them, holding his double-barreled barn blaster up high across his shoulders, a Colt .44 slung low on his right hip. He had a Smith & Wesson wedged behind the big gold buckle of his shell belt.

"I sure coulda used that beer," he growled as the lead

rider threw up his gloved right hand and checked his rangy sorrel gelding down in front of the jailhouse.

The riders behind him, most of whom wore dusters and plenty of pistols on their grim-faced, gimlet-eyed persons, did likewise, all firing wild, angry looks toward the veranda. Arroyo Simms rode a steel dust stallion, his eyes beneath his broad hat brim spoked with humor. The yellow-haired Lou Savage, who'd been riding directly behind the old gent, now moved up to sit his coyote dun beside him. The older man raked his sharp, pale blue gaze across the three law bringers several times before, holding the reins of his restless mount up taut against his chest, he let his eyes settle on Longarm.

"I understand my son was kidnapped from his favorite watering hole last evening." The dust caught up to Norvell Wade, and he blinked against it, his nut brown, clean-shaven cheeks hardening as he set his jaws as though to temper his rage. "You the one did the kidnappin'?"

"Your son wasn't kidnapped, Mr. Wade. He was arrested. He'll be headin' back to Denver with me, Deputy U.S. Marshal Custis Long, to stand trial for the murder of three sheriff's deputies and a shotgunner riding for the U.S. Mail."

Arroyo Simms laughed, throwing his head back on his shoulders.

Wade gritted his teeth and closed his right hand over the carved horn grips of his long-barreled, silver-plated .44 jutting from a black holster on his right thigh, which was clad in black wool trousers and brush-scarred bull-hide chaps. Longarm snapped up his Winchester and loudly racked a fresh round into the breech.

Wade's eyes flashed silver daggers, but he kept the horn-gripped gun in its holster.

Simms stopped laughing.

"You're under arrest, Wade," Longarm growled down the barrel of his Winchester. "You, too, Savage, Simms. And all the rest of you men. Throw down them guns—and I mean every one—or I'll shoot you deader'n fence posts."

Simms chuckled but his heart wasn't it.

Both Buckshot Pete and Jessie glanced at Longarm. Wade glowered at the rifle-wielding lawman so hard that Longarm thought the man's pale blue eyes would pop right out of his head.

"On what charge?" Wade roared.

"You're pissin' me off, and I don't like it."

Lou Savage, wearing a black duster, had his own right hand on one of the two pistols on his hips. He jerked a confounded look at his boss. "See there, Mr. Wade. The man just ain't reasonable. He seems to make up the rules as he goes, like he was Jesus H. Christ his own self. Personally, I think he's plum loco." He grinned as he looked back at Longarm, slanting his devilish green eyes. "Needs puttin' down like a crazy old dog."

"I asked you what the charge was," Wade roared again.

"Now you can add vagrancy to the list." Longarm grinned with menace at Savage. "I'm gonna ask you just once to lift your hand from that hogleg's grips and dismount. We only got four cells, so it's gonna get a mite crowded, but we'll make do. Maybe one or two of you can sing for us tonight."

Wesley Wade's voice rose from inside the jailhouse. "Be careful, Pa, he's crazy. Just like Lou says. He done brained me good—once from behind, then once as he was leadin' me into the jailhouse. For no good reason." Young

Wade's voice broke. "Pa, you gotta get me outta here. I don't think he's fixin' to take me to Denver at all. He wants to finish me hisself!"

Longarm glanced at Wade, but someone on the rancher's far left moved suddenly—a stocky rider in a red-checked neckerchief—jerking a big Schofield out of a shoulder rig under his salmon duster. Longarm slid his Winchester two feet, and the explosion echoed around the morning-quiet street, flatting out over the rooftops toward the surrounding ridges.

The stocky rider screamed as, dropping the Schofield, he clutched his bloody right wrist, his fleshy face crumpling with agony as he cast a shocked, infuriated look at Longarm. The federal lawman hoped that wounding the man would stay the others, but he hadn't yet racked a fresh round in the Winchester's chamber before both Savage and Norvell Wade slapped leather. A half second later, the rest of the riders, including Arroyo Simms, were reaching for guns in the periphery of Longarm's vision.

Quickly, he drew a bead on Savage; the Winchester roared and leaped in his hands.

"Ugh!" Savage said, jerking back in his saddle, then dropping his gaze to the hole spurting blood in his upper left chest. He dropped his pistol and started to slap a hand to the hole in his chest, but his horse wheeled sharply and tossed the man out of his saddle.

He hit the street groaning and rolling, dying fast.

"Fuck!" Arroyo Simms shouted. "You're one crazy sonofabitch, Longarm!"

Suddenly, as Buckshot Pete triggered one of the barrels of his double-bore, the floorboards leaping beneath Longarm's boots at the cannonlike explosion, all hell was breaking loose. One of the riders to the right of Norvell Wade, targeted by Buckshot Pete, cursed loudly as he triggered his big Colt at the jailhouse veranda and turned bright red as he was thrown back off his screaming buckskin as though he'd been lassoed from the vestibule of a train tearing away behind him.

A rider beside him clutched his arm as part of the buckshot load punched into his left side and poked a couple of nasty, bright red holes in his cheek.

As a slug plowed into the awning support post beside him and another screamed over his head and into the front of the jailhouse, Longarm quickly triggered his Winchester four more times, shooting and levering, empty cartridge casings careening over his right shoulder to dance around on the veranda floor. As much lead as he punched toward the jostling group obscured by their own powder smoke, he didn't think he'd hit more than one rider more after Savage, possibly two. They were all pitching around too wildly, some turning complete circles on their screaming, wide-eyed mounts.

Jessie was down on both knees on the far side of Buckshot Pete, calmly triggering her Winchester from her shoulder, her empty cartridge casings *ping*ing off the board bench against the jailhouse wall behind her.

Buckshot Pete discharged his gut shredder's second barrel to the demise of a big redheaded hombre who'd been firing two pistols from the saddle of his steel dust stallion but who now flopped wildly down his horse's hip as the animal crow-hopped and wheeled, flinging its rider far and wide into the street and went screaming back in the direction from which it had come, into the sifting dust of two other riderless ranch ponies.

"Retreat, men—*retreat!*" Norvell Wade shouted beneath the roaring gunfire as, sporting a bloody gash across the side of his neck, the rancher reined his own horse around and put the steel to it.

Longarm held fire as the riders who'd remained in their saddles, including the loudly cursing Arroyo Simms, wheeled their mounts and booted them hard after their retreating boss. Several hunched low, wounded, while one man triggered a revolver over his shoulder as he put his speckle-black after the others, jumping Lou Savage, who now lay twisted and still in the street before the jailhouse.

Jessie, who'd ceased firing to thumb fresh shells into her Winchester's breech, racked a live round and aimed straight out from her shoulder, squinting down the rifle's barrel at the gunmen retreating behind a cloud of dust and powder smoke. Longarm reached over and grabbed the rifle just as she triggered it, sending the slug screeching off over the rooftops of Santiago.

"Hold up, girl," Longarm ordered. "Not even Wade's worth back-shooting."

Jessie jerked her rifle back angrily. "I say we take down as many as we can. Wade'll be back with more."

"Not many more," Buckshot Pete said, breeching his shotgun and plucking spent wads from the two large, round, smoking barrels. "He don't have all that many more gunslicks on his roll than what we seen right here. He's got plenty of range riders—mostly scrub Meskins who couldn't find work south of the border. But all these he brought to town're pistoleers, and now ole Lou Savage is dead. He's still got Simms, but shit . . ."

The sheriff closed his big shotgun and, adjusting his belly gun, stepped a little unsteadily into the street, heading for the man slumped closest to the jailhouse. Longarm headed for the next one out while Jessie waited on the veranda's top step, looking rankled as she stared after the riders who'd disappeared, though their hoof thuds could still be heard echoing into the distance.

Buckshot Pete kicked over the man he'd walked to. "Chisos Owens. Southern California gunslinger. My gut-shredder didn't leave much of him to bury." He looked over at Longarm, who'd kicked over another man lying dead near Savage. "Who you got there?"

"I'll be damned," Longarm muttered. "This appears to be Bear Kuhn out of Salt Lake. I heard he died pret' near five years ago now in Abilene, Kansas."

"I told you that'll happen around here," Buckshot said, shambling past Longarm toward the third dead man, who lay on his side in the middle of the broad street. "Men who you thought been pushin' up sage and tilted tombstones for a good long time suddenly make an appearance—a little older, a little owlier . . ."

Buckshot suddenly dropped to both his knees and vomited.

"Pa!" Jessie dumped down the steps.

Buckshot held up a hand as he retched once more. Sucking a ragged breath, he said, "Oh, I'll be all right in a minute. Reckon it's the heat and the powder smoke. Fetch me a beer, will ya, girl?"

Jessie wheeled and ran back into the jailhouse while Longarm looked around, making sure no one else was wanting in on the action, which often happened in dust-ups, blood and powder smoke being a heady elixir. Several people were pushing out from the shops and into the street, including a man with a dusty top hat wearing round spectacles over his hungry, dung brown eyes.

Doubtless, the undertaker, who, hearing the gunfire, had come out to see about business. He limped over to

Lou Savage, whistling softly, then picked up his pace as he ran over to another dead man bleeding out in the street.

Looking toward the hotel, Longarm saw Raquella Mayfair edging cautiously along the edge of the hotel's red-board veranda, one hand on a support post, the other shielding her eyes as she stared toward the scene of the shooting. She wore a simple housedress, but no dress looked simple on a girl with her curves. Several men in the customarily gaudy attire of gamblers had come out to inspect the situation as well. Longarm thought he heard Malcolm yelling from inside the lobby, but it couldn't be. With his badly broken leg, the Southern dandy had to be passed out upstairs, snuggled up to several empty brandy bottles.

Hector Padilla came out, followed by his matronly wife, who had a towel slung over her shoulder. Padilla was gritting his teeth dreadfully while his wife shook her head in disapproval, crossing her arms over her matronly chest.

Satisfied he wasn't about to be bushwhacked by some drunk ranny infected with the lead fever, Longarm kicked over the fourth man down in the street. Not recognizing the shooter, he glanced over his shoulder at Buckshot Pete, who hungrily grabbed the brown beer bottle out of his daughter's outstretched hand.

"Big man with a star tattooed into his right cheek." Longarm looked down at the dead man again, nudging his head from side to side with a boot toe. "A moon tattooed into the other one."

Buckshot Pete lowered the beer bottle, the foamy fluid running down his unshaven chin, and sighed. "Edgar Lavuto?"

The sheriff shook his head. Jessie helped him to his

feet, and, holding his beer bottle with its ceramic flip-top hanging down from the lip, he tramped with his daughter over to Longarm and looked down at the fourth dead man, who had one eye shot out and the back of his head turned to mush.

"Sure enough—Edgar Lavuto. Shit, ole Wade's got him quite a string of shooters. No tellin' who he's got back at the ranch, but I got me a feelin' we're in for a mighty nasty surprise."

"Thought you said he don't have that many," Jessie said.

"It ain't the number," Buckshot Pete said, then took another long pull from the beer. "It's the quality. And if the rest are anything like Lavuto here, we got some mighty big guns headed our way."

Longarm sighed as he studied the dead men then stared off in the direction in which the others had fled.

Jessie sidled up to him, squinting at him skeptically. "Was you really thinkin' you were gonna arrest that bunch, Custis?"

"Nah. I could tell those boys thought they could get us on the run, and I wanted to make sure they learned better *mas* pronto. We might have some seasoned shooters headed our way again, but they'll be more careful next time, and maybe they won't be in such a rush."

Jessie stared up at him, pressing her lips together and dimpling her cheeks. Longarm gave her a grin, and jerked her hat brim down. "How's our prisoner?"

"He's sittin' on his cot lookin' none too happy. He probably saw what happened to his pa's gunnies through the windows. Lucky for us he didn't catch a stray slug," she said with faint sarcasm. "The front windows were all shot out."

"Yeah, we wouldn't want to lose him."

Longarm glanced at Buckshot, who was beginning to regain some color in his cheeks. "Wade likely won't be back for a while," said Longarm. "I think I'll head on over to the hotel and get a drink and a meal, maybe even a bath and a few winks. Wanna be fresh for after sundown. Can you two watch the jail till I spell you? Someone oughta be over there at all times until the cavalry comes to our rescue."

Buckshot nodded. "I reckon I done rested enough, past few weeks." Tipping the beer bottle back, he stomped off toward the jailhouse while the undertaker strode busily amongst the dead men, digging into pockets and pulling out coins and watches and inspecting blood-splattered six-shooters. A dusty brown dog joined him, sniffing Chisos Owens's shredded belly.

"You goin' over to the Red Ridge Inn?" Jessie asked Longarm.

"That's where I'm holed up."

"That's where Mrs. Mayfair's holed up, too, ain't it?"

"Yep." Longarm gave a wry snort and, resting his rifle on his shoulder, headed for the hotel.

Only Hector Padilla remained on the veranda, Raquella and the gamblers having retreated into the hotel.

As Longarm mounted the hotel's veranda, Padilla crossed himself and muttered a quick prayer. "The Wade riders . . ." the Mexican whispered awfully. "They are very bad men. If Señor Wade is not too seriously injured, he will return. He and Arroyo Simms. They may have underestimated you, señor . . ."

". . . call me Longarm."

"They may have underestimated your abilities and

the size of your cojones here today." Padilla shook his head. "But next time, they will not be so easy to run off."

"Señor Padilla," Longarm said, staring at the man, "you're startin' to get on my nerves."

Padilla's flushed face slackened.

Longarm turned away from the man and tramped into the hotel.

Chapter 15

As Longarm crossed the lobby to the stairs, he heard a familiar voice and turned to gaze into the hotel's dining room/saloon. He was amazed to see Malcolm Mayfair sitting at a table near the bar with the gamblers whom Longarm had seen with Raquella out on the hotel's veranda a few minutes ago, investigating the dustup in front of the jailhouse.

Mayfair sat in a rickety-looking wheelchair sideways to the table, his right leg sheathed in plaster of Paris suspended on a metal and wood brace extended straight out in front of him. His bare toes protruding from the plaster cast were swollen and purple, but the dandy didn't seem to mind. He was thoroughly embroiled in the stud game that he and the other men had going beneath a thick cloud of tobacco smoke. His alcohol-thick Southern drawl fairly echoed around the room as he called out bets and badgered the other badgering, guffawing gamblers between deep drinks from a half-filled snifter.

Longarm looked around.

No sign of Raquella. She was probably up in their room. He ignored the tug in his loins—he needed rest, not more dalliance with a married woman—and called to Hector Padilla to have a bath sent up, then mounted the stairs, clomping like a blown-out old horse. His shoulders were heavy, his legs creaky. He'd gone too long without sleep, food, or drink, and he needed all soon but a bath and a few hours of shut-eye first.

On the second floor, he walked past the Mayfairs' closed door on the way to his own room, noting the silence behind it but then turning his mind away from it. *Sleep*, he told himself . . .

After he'd fumbled his own door open and opened a window to air the musty place out, he undressed slowly, wearily, tossing his dusty, sweat-soaked duds on the floor. He was sitting on the bed with a towel over his lap, his holstered .44 beside him, when a knock sounded.

"Come in," he yawned.

"Open the door, *por favor*," said the woman's vaguely familiar, taut, breathless voice.

Longarm cursed, rose, and, wrapping the towel around his waist, tramped barefoot to the door and threw it open. He frowned, then stepped back as Raquella pushed past him, lugging two steaming wooden buckets in her hands.

"Good Lord, woman!" Longarm corkscrewed his face with exasperation. "What the hell are you doing?"

"What does it look like?" Raquella set the buckets down with a grunt, then straightened, her cheeks flushed from exertion. Her hair was tumbling free from the bun atop her head; it jostled down her cheeks, thick chocolate curls caressing her neck.

She swept an especially thick lock of it back from her

forehead and cast her brown-eyed gaze at Longarm. "Room twelve needs a bath, no?"

"What're you doin' fetching it?"

"I work here now," she said in her thick Mexican accent. "We are broke. Or nearly broke. What little we have left Malcolm will soon lose downstairs or drink up in brandy. I am working to pay for the room and meals until Malcolm is well enough to travel."

"Hell, you shoulda asked me. I would have—"

"No," Raquella said, cutting him off and walking over to him, wrapping her arms around his waist and looking up into his face with a weary smile. "I would feel like a whore. I do not wish to feel like a whore. A woman, yes. Not a whore." She pressed her cheek against his chest. "I am glad you are not hurt. That was some dustup, even by Méjico standards."

"It was a pretty good dustup even by my own standards." Longarm ran his hand through her thick hair, pressing her head against his chest. "You see any more of it, you make sure you stay inside and keep your head down. I'd hate to see such a pretty one get shot off."

He tipped her chin up with his fingers and kissed her. She lifted her arms from his waist to his neck and clung to him desperately, returning the kiss. After a long time, she pulled away, running the back of her hand across her mouth.

"Your bath . . ." She turned and strode to the open door, glancing at him over her shoulder with a wicked little grin. "I'll be right back with the tub, and then we'll see about getting you cleaned up."

She winked and went out.

Longarm sagged back onto the bed, feeling that tug in his loins again. It was a much harder pull this time,

and he knew he couldn't sleep now if he threw back an
entire bottle of laudanum. He heard a door in the hall
open. There was a tinny rattle, then the closet door
slammed closed. His own door opened, and Raquella
walked in dragging a tarnished copper bathtub. She
kicked the door closed, then poured the steaming water
from one of the buckets into the tub.

"This one's hot," she said and set the empty bucket
on the floor.

She took up the second bucket and poured it, too, into
the copper tub.

"This one's lukewarm."

When she'd set the second bucket down on the floor,
she straightened and planted her fists on her hips, her
eyes turning smoky. "Come. I will wash you, Custis."

Longarm looked down at his lap. His dong tented the
towel draped over his thighs. A little embarrassing, since
she was still fully clothed, but he'd endured far worse hu-
miliations. He looked at her simple, low-cut housedress, at
the small, silver crucifix nestled in her deep, tan cleavage,
and his temples throbbed.

"You sure we ain't gonna be interrupted?"

"Sí, I'm sure. I am due for a break soon. Señor and
Señora Padilla will probably think I have taken it. As for
Malcolm—he is too busy losing our money." Raquella
extended her hand. "Throw me the towel and come over
here. I will wash you, rub the weariness from your muscles."

Longarm pushed himself to his feet and removed the
towel. His throbbing cock jutted nearly straight up in the
air. Raquella dropped her eyes to it, and her throat
moved as she swallowed. He threw the towel to her, and
as he walked over to the tub, she tossed the towel over

her shoulder, whispering, "*Mierda.* You are one lovely hombre."

Longarm stepped into the tub. The water was just right, almost too hot, and he dropped down into it with a weary, luxurious groan and rested his hands on the built-in armrests. "Damn, that feels good." He looked at the dresser, where his nickel cheroots rested near his badge and wallet. "Only one thing would make it better."

Raquella chuckled softly. "A cigar?"

"You wouldn't mind?"

Raquella walked over to the dresser, grabbed one of the cheroots, and, turning back to face Longarm, stuck the cigar between her ripe, sexy lips. She removed a stove match from atop the dresser, scratched it to life on a drawer handle, and touched the flame to the cigar's round tip.

Puffing smoke and narrowing her eyes, she walked back to him, knelt down beside the tub, removed the cigar from between her lips, wrapped an arm brusquely around his neck, and kissed him long and hard. She groaned and snaked her tongue down his throat.

Then she pulled away and held out the cigar.

He took it and, feeling the cooler air of the room caress the mushroom head of his cock as it jutted above the steaming water, placed the cheroot between his teeth. As she leaned over to grab a sponge from off the bottom of the tub, between his legs and just in front of his piston-hard member, her dress fell away from her chest.

Her breasts sloped outward, rich and swollen, the nipples hardening behind the rough cotton fabric.

She scrubbed him slowly, starting with the back of his neck, his ears, his back, shoulders, and arms. Then under his arms and his chest and belly, once or twice nudging his cock with the sponge but otherwise leaving it alone. As she cleaned out his belly button, she stuck her warm, wet tongue in his ear, then briefly nibbled his lobe.

Meanwhile, he puffed the cigar and watched her breasts jostle the way they'd jumped and tossed in the ill-fated stage.

His dong remained so hard he was half-certain the skin would split. The water splashed over and around it. A couple of times she squeezed out the soapy sponge on it, and he sighed and gripped the sides of the tub hard with his hands and clamped down on his cigar.

Last, she washed his cock and balls. She scrubbed him the way a nurse would do it, purposefully, expertly, tenderly while seemingly oblivious of his raging hard-on, her hair jostling down across her breasts as she worked, singing softly to herself in Spanish.

When she was finally done washing him, she plucked the cigar from his teeth and ordered him to stand and dry himself. She stood near the tub watching him, puffing the cigar between her own sensuous lips. When he was almost through with the drying, she grabbed the towel, shoved him down on the side of the bed, and finished drying each of his legs.

She tossed the towel behind her. She plucked the cigar from her rich lips and handed it to him.

"Now," she said raspily, "the finish."

She pulled her hair back from her face, lowered her head over his dong, and took him so far down her throat that he thought he could feel her heart beating while his own nearly burst.

When she pulled the tub out of the room several minutes later and Longarm had climbed into bed, clean and sated and ready for a nap, she blew him a kiss. Longarm caught the kiss in the air and looked over the bottom of the bed at the half-open door she was sidestepping through.

Boots thumped, and someone appeared in the hall near Raquella. Longarm's heart skipped an embarrassed beat as he saw Jessie's tawny hair tumbling over slender shoulders. The girl was apparently heading for her own room, her rifle in one hand, saddlebags on her other shoulder.

She stopped and looked at Raquella, then slid her suspicious gaze into the room, her eyes meeting Longarm's, and narrowing.

"Marshal Long," Raquella said with an oblique smile, "wanted a bath."

She closed the door.

"I'll just bet he did," Longarm heard Jessie say in the hall.

He dropped his head against his pillow with a groan.

Still, it wasn't long before sleep washed over him.

A gunshot woke him. It was a loud blast, like a double-barreled shotgun.

He jerked his head up, blinking.

Another thundering boom. A woman screamed, and a dog started barking.

Pete . . .

Longarm swung out of bed so fast he nearly passed out. The light angling through the windows was the soft gold of early evening. He'd slept longer than he'd intended. When he'd steadied himself on the dresser and the room had stopped bouncing around him, he looked around for his clothes. They were all piled neatly on a chair. Apparently, Raquella had retrieved them, washed and dried them, folded them, and returned them to his room while he'd sawed logs.

Christ, he'd been tired . . .

Hearing the dog barking more wildly on the street below his window and a man shouting on the heels of two
quick pistol shots, Longarm threw his clothes on, stomped
into his boots, and, hitching his shell belt around his
waist, ran out into the hall as the shotgun boomed once
more. He almost collided with Jessie, who was jogging
past his room, looking sleep-bleary and strapping her own
cartridge belt around her waist.

"That's Pa's barn blaster," she said as they tramped
quickly together down the carpeted hall.

"I got a feelin' he ain't shootin' at quail."

They ran down the stairs and across the lobby. The
Padillas had gathered at the front door and were looking
out into the street. A claybank mare was angling toward
the hotel veranda, and as Longarm stepped between the
Padillas and onto the porch, with Jessie on his heels, he
saw that the horse had a rider.

The man was flopping around on the horse's back,
barely able to keep his head up. In his hand was a long,
smoking Colt. Longarm palmed his own .44-40 but held
fire as the man dropped his pistol into the street. He had
a broad, bearded face and deep-set, pain-racked eyes.
His checked shirt behind a doeskin vest was blood bibbed.
As the horse approached the veranda, sort of sidestepping
and nickering nervously, the man gave a groan and rolled
out of the saddle. He hit the street with a thud, a groan,
and a fart.

His eyes turned glassy as he stared straight up at the
desert green sky.

Longarm looked back toward the jailhouse a block
away and on the other side of the street. Between the
hotel and the jail, Buckshot Pete stood breeching his

Winchester and plucking the spent wads from the barrels. He was looking around cautiously as though for more shooters.

Spreading out and walking abreast, Longarm and Jessie walked toward him, both with their guns out and looking around.

"Had me a couple of visitors while you two was off in dreamland," Buckshot Pete said, snapping his shotgun closed.

Longarm wheeled slowly. "Where's the other one?"

"On the jailhouse porch."

"The one by the hotel is Roamy Slaven," Jessie said. "What in the world . . . ?"

When Longarm saw no other possible bushwhackers, he walked toward the jailhouse, in front of which the collie dog was still barking angrily.

"Git, Henry," Jessie ordered as she, Longarm, and her father approached the sheriff's office. "Git on home!"

The dog groaned, then ran off around the far side of the jailhouse and out of sight.

Longarm stopped near the hitchrack. A man lay sprawled belly-up, limbs akimbo, on the jailhouse veranda. He was stocky and gray-bearded with a big paunch, and he wore a green-checked shirt under a buckskin vest that had been shredded by Buckshot Pete's double-bore shotgun. A steeple-crowned sombrero lay in the dirt just off the veranda's front step.

"Ralph Montoya," said Buckshot Pete, caressing his still-smoking shotgun as though it were a long and trusted friend. "Him and Roamy Slaven rode for Jim Wells over to Crystal Creek. A couple of raggedy-heeled punchers who spent most of their time in the saloons here in Santiago."

"I don't understand, Pa," Jessie said, casting her worried gaze from Montoya's sprawling form to that of Slaven over by the hotel. "They don't work for the Wades."

"No, but they probably figured they'd get good money for busting Wade's son out of the hoosegow." Longarm holstered his .44 and looked around the darkening street once more.

From the other side of town, someone was strumming a Mexican guitar. It was getting dark over there. Dark and quiet. The lights from the cantinas shone dully along the crooked street.

"We're gonna have to be extra careful, these next few days," he said. "It's not only the Wades we gotta worry about, but any thirty-and-found-puncher who might get liquored up and decide to do some moonlighting."

He turned to Buckshot Pete. "You're still pretty good with that big popper of your'n."

Having reloaded the gun, Buckshot snapped it closed. He held it in one hand, held the other hand out before him. It was shaking. His face was pasty, and the soft evening light gilded the sweat beads running down his cheeks.

"Few more days, I'll be good as new." He swung around and, stepping over the dead man on the porch, hurried into the jailhouse.

Longarm looked at Jessie. She looked back at him, and heaved a worried sigh.

Chapter 16

The night passed with no shootings and only one stabbing in Santiago, and that was a short-lived disagreement between two vaqueros over a buxom girl on the Mexican side of town. Longarm and Buckshot Pete arbitrated the dustup, and it ended with the victim being sewn up by a Mexican sawbones. Afterward, the victim and his attacker rode back out to their rancho singing a sentimental ballad and passing a bottle of bacanora back and forth between themselves.

The buxom girl had long since disappeared.

There was no sign of the Wade bunch in town that night. And no others fishing for bounty money came gunning for Longarm, Jessie, or Buckshot Pete. In the jailhouse, all was quiet. Wade slept off his twice-battered head with his face in his pillow.

Since Longarm was the most capable of the three law bringers, he patrolled the town with either Jessie or her father, who took turns staying in the locked jailhouse

with Wade, aiming either a cocked rifle or a shotgun at
the stone building's stout oak door.

Din from the saloons and cantinas and the Red Ridge
Saloon died around three A.M. The stars wheeled, sparkling crisply in the dry desert sky. Coyotes howled the
sun up, and the heat returned like a vast blanket. The
tang of spiced goat meat rose on the smoke from breakfast fires.

Longarm was out on the veranda, drinking coffee and
smoking, when he heard Buckshot Pete stir in his chair
behind his battered desk, where he'd dozed off and on
all night. Jessie was asleep in one of the empty cells.

"All quiet out there, Custis?"

Longarm sat on the porch rail, surveying the main
street that the soft desert sun was slowly revealing while
slowly dissolving shadows and illuminating the high,
false fronts of the business buildings. A few minutes ago,
he'd watched a lobo slink out of an alley mouth and
cross the street with a large cow bone it had scavenged
from a trash heap and head off into the desert.

"All quiet. Too damn quiet."

"Figured it'd be that way."

Buckshot Pete scuffed out the open door behind him,
pulling his suspenders over his shoulders and adjusting
them over his slight paunch. He cradled his shotgun in
one arm, his beer bottle in the other. He'd taken a few
sips from the bottle all night, just to relieve the shakes,
but Longarm didn't think he'd had more than one entire
beer and maybe a few sips from a second one.

"You're doin' all right, Pete," he said, appraising his
old friend, noting the color in his cheeks. The sheriff
didn't seem to be sweating as much anymore, either.

Buckshot Pete sighed. "I tell you, Custis, I'd rather

fight a bobcat in the boot of a runaway Concord coach than go through what I been goin' through. That office floor was aslither all night with snakes." He ran a paw down his face. "I'm a damn fool. Been a fool in front of you and my girl in there. I'm just sorry she had to see my true colors. Before Spring dumped me, I'd managed to keep my drinkin' down to just while card playin' every other night or so. I swear, though"—he gave Longarm a hard, unwavering look—"my drinkin' days are over. If I survive Wade, I'm gonna put in another year or two here as the sheriff of San Isabel County—a sober year or two—just to prove I'm still good enough, and to squirrel away a nest egg for myself and Jessie. Then I'm gonna retire, maybe move on up to Phoenix or Prescott and get a business of some sort."

Longarm blew a smoke plume into the street and quirked a mouth corner with a wry smile. "You're gonna make it, Pete. You've already proven it to me. Now you just gotta prove it to yourself."

"And that girl in there." Buckshot looked down at his badly worn and ratty undershirt and duck pants, both knees of which were nearly worn through. "Look at me. Christ, I used to be a right smart dresser. Can you watch over things here while I go on over and get a bath at the Chinaman's place? I need a good long soak in his hot springs, and to get into some decent duds."

"I don't reckon we gotta worry about Wade comin' for a while. Hell, he might be too badly wounded to come. Go on and have your soak. Take your time." Longarm arched a brow. "Just watch your back, Pete. There's a chance some of the Chain Link boys slipped into town overnight, left their horses out in the desert."

"I know that, Custis. My brain ain't totally pickled."

With that, Buckshot Pete swiped his hat playfully across Longarm's knee, then, hiking his shotgun on his shoulder, stepped heavily off the porch and sauntered out into the street, angling east. Longarm went inside the jailhouse for another cup of the coffee simmering on the black, bullet-shaped cookstove, then tramped back out to the veranda to drink it and finish his cheroot.

He thought over the situation. There was a possibility that yesterday's dustup out here had been the end of Wade's attempt to free his son from the jail. A slim one, but a chance nonetheless. When Wade had galloped away, he'd been holding a hand over his bloody neck. At Wade's age—late sixties, at least—that might have been enough to discourage the man.

Of course, he could remain at the ranch and send his riders. He hadn't hired Simms and the other veteran pistoleers just for show.

No, he'd at least send them, all right. Sooner or later.

Longarm tossed his cheroot stub into the dusty street and hoped that Simms might be injured badly enough that he'd delay another attack by Wade until after the soldiers had been through Santiago. It was probably too much to hope for, but it gave the federal badge toter a light optimism, anyway. He wasn't sure how long or how effectively he, Jessie, and Buckshot Pete could hold off the storm of Wade's seasoned shooters. Just Longarm, a salty girl, and an old town tamer whose best town taming was years ago . . .

Buckshot Pete might have given up the bottle, but after the amount of liquor he'd been consuming over the past few months, his nerves had to be shot. Longarm hated to admit it to himself, but he couldn't depend on the man. And while Jessie was as tough a girl as he'd ever known, she didn't have the experience. The three of them would make a fight of it, but Wade's pistoleers were just too good and too many.

There was little doubt who would win.

Longarm realized he'd been hearing voices behind him when Wesley Wade shouted, "Hold on, girl! Hold on! I was just funnin'!"

Longarm stepped through the jailhouse door as Jessie cocked her Winchester loudly and, standing in front of Wade's cell door, raised the carbine to her shoulder. Wade threw his hands up high and stepped back, his face pinched with terror.

"You can't shoot an unarmed man through a cell door. Longarm! Help!"

Longarm moved into the room, making a beeline for Jessie, who glanced over her shoulder and grinned, depressing the Winchester's hammer. "Don't worry—I wasn't really gonna shoot him. I just wanted to hear him scream like the girl he is and watch him piss down his leg."

"What's this about?" Longarm said, shuttling his glance between her and Wade, who kept his fear-bright eyes on the Winchester-wielding deputy.

"I was just funnin' the girl," Wade intoned.

"He asked me if I'd drop my jeans and sit on his face," Jessie said, lowering the Winchester. "I told him that was no way to talk to a lady and didn't his ma ever teach him no manners. He told me I should go in there and teach him while sittin' on his face, and I asked him how he'd like a forty-four pill drilled through his teeth." She set the rifle on her shoulder. "That's all."

"You're quite the charmer—ain't ya, Wade?" Longarm said, chuckling as he moved over to the woodstove with his empty coffee cup.

"You ain't no lady," Wade said, stepping back up close to the cell door, keeping his angry gaze on Jessie. "No woman would talk the way you do or dress all the time in them rags. And just for what you just done, aimin' that gun on me, I'm gonna make sure you pay dear when my pa rides in with his pistoleers. And don't think a little neck graze is gonna keep him away. Hell, he's probably already here, surrounding the jailhouse and bidin' his time."

"Shut up, Wade," Longarm warned as he refilled his coffee cup with the black, piping-hot brew. "Or I'm gonna let Jessie take you to the dance with her Winchester."

"Love to." Jessie smirked at Wade, who backed away from the cell door once more, apprehension furling his dark brows.

Jessie leaned her rifle against the wall near the door, yawning, and plucked a coffee cup off a shelf near the stove. She filled the cup, then followed Longarm back out onto the porch, where he took up his position again on the rail.

"Did you enjoy your bath yesterday?" she asked, blowing into her cup and not looking at him.

"Yeah. It was good and hot."

"I'll bet it was."

Longarm chuckled and looked around at the street turning buttery as the sun climbed higher. Wagons and horseback riders were moving now, ranchmen and miners taking advantage of the coolness of morning to get their town chores done.

"Where's Pa?" Jessie asked.

"Went for a bath at the Chinaman's place."

"'Bout time. He smells like a horse that rolled in a whiskey vat."

"Why don't you go on over to the hotel and get yourself some breakfast? I'll stay here with Wade."

"Sure you wouldn't rather go?" Jessie arched a brow at Longarm. "Mrs. Mayfair might be working in the dining room this morning."

Longarm glowered at her. "Quit moonin'. You got what you wanted, same as me. Now, run along and get some breakfast. We likely got a long day of waiting ahead. Bring me back a plate."

When Jessie had grabbed her rifle and set her cup inside the jailhouse, she walked back out onto the veranda, setting her Stetson on her head and sweeping her hair back behind her shoulders. She glanced at Longarm, her eyes sharp. "I ain't just some girl you can order around, you know."

Longarm winked at her. "I reckon I found that out in the desert. In more ways than one."

Jessie's lips quirked a begrudging half smile as she tramped down the porch steps, her spurs ringing, her rifle on her shoulder, and headed along the street toward the Red Ridge Inn. She swung her taut, round rump behind those skin-tight denims, and Longarm enjoyed every minute of it.

After she'd returned from the hotel, bringing him a plate of ham, eggs, and potatoes, and he'd finished it along with another cup of a coffee and a postbreakfast cheroot, he started to worry about Buckshot Pete. It was nearly ten o'clock, and the Santiago sheriff hadn't returned from his bath.

Jessie was inside at the desk while Longarm lounged on the veranda abutting the building's front wall. "How long can your pa linger in a bath?"

She must have been worried as well. She stepped outside and looked along the street, resting a hand on a roof post. "He can linger all day if he's drunk. He damn near drowned over there about a month ago. The Chinaman caught him just in time."

"He wouldn't linger today."

"Not if he didn't start drinkin' again. I don't think he'd take this long even if he was gettin' some new duds over to the mercantile on credit."

Longarm grabbed his Winchester from against the wall. "I'm gonna take a stroll. You stay here, keep the door locked. Don't let anyone in. And don't give me any shit about you not bein' a girl who takes orders."

"I wasn't going to," she snapped.

"Good." Longarm stepped off the veranda and looked eastward along the mostly deserted street. "Is the Chinaman's place just past the hotel, on a side street?"

Jessie said it was, and Longarm continued up the main street, hugging the shade under brush arbors from where he could more easily pick out would-be bushwhackers. He hadn't gone much past the hotel before he stopped suddenly.

Three small Mexican boys in crude, soiled white pajamas and rope-soled sandals were running toward him. One of the boys held a shotgun in his hands, the gun so heavy for the lad that he couldn't quite keep up with the others. The one carrying the gun wore a straw sombrero several sizes too big for him.

Longarm stared at the shotgun in the kid's hands. The gun grew larger as the group approached. His heart thudded.

The trio tried to run around him but he stepped into

their path, holding up his hands, palm out. "Hold on, fellas. *Alto!* What you got there?"

In Spanish that he was able to decipher despite the speed with which they all spoke at the same time, the boys told him some gringo with a bandage on his neck gave the shotgun to them with orders that they deliver it to the sheriff's office. In his own cow-pen Spanish, Longarm managed to get across to the boys that he was the one to whom the shotgun had been meant to be delivered.

He gave each boy a silver dollar, and when they'd run off, yelling and tossing the coins in the air, Longarm held up the shotgun in his hands. It was a simple popper, well-worn but clean, and it smelled of the gun oil Buckshot Pete had lovingly applied to it the night before.

A wad of white paper protruded from the end of the left barrel.

Looking around warily, Longarm plucked the paper from the barrel and shook it out one-handed. On the lined notepaper was penciled: "You want Buckshot Peckinpah back? Bring my son to the old church on the Mex side of town at high noon."

At the bottom of the page, the Chain Link brand was scrawled in heavy pencil.

Chapter 17

"I sure am sorry about this, you two," mocked Wesley Wade as Longarm and Jessie led the young firebrand out of the jailhouse and into the street. "Here, you really thought you had me squirreled away safe and sound, just waitin' on the soldiers. When was they comin'—tomorrow?"

"Shut up, Wade," Jessie said.

"One more word, Wade," Longarm said, "and you're gonna have a goose egg on your right temple to match the one on your left."

Longarm had a leather noose he'd fashioned from a horse harness around Wesley's neck. He'd made a second, much smaller loop in which he'd attached the barrel of his Winchester, so the maw of the rifle was snugged up tight against the back of Wade's neck, just above his shirt collar.

Wade turned his head to glance over his shoulder at Longarm. "You can't do nothin' to me without endangerin' old Buckshot."

Longarm jerked the end of the harness taut in his left hand. Wade's face reddened as the leather drew snug around his neck, and he choked, rasping, "All right, all right!"

Longarm slackened the noose and kicked the firebrand forward so hard that Wesley was nearly driven to his knees. He ground his jaws, but, getting his footing under himself once more, said nothing as he continued walking.

The sun was high, burning into the street. Longarm had his shirtsleeves down to keep the sun out, but he could feel sweat dribbling along his spine. His string tie flopped loose around his neck. He wore his deputy U.S. marshal's badge pinned to his breast pocket so that there would be no question who Wade's men would be shooting at, trying to kill. And there was no doubt that lead would be flying soon.

Longarm intended to get Buckshot Pete back safely in addition to keeping Wesley under wraps. He'd arrest any of the men he'd find behind the church, too—or as many as possible. Those he didn't kill, that is. Norvell Wade's shooters were all now nearly as incriminated as the young hard case they'd been conspiring to set free.

Longarm kept shifting his eyes from one side of the street to the other. Hardly anyone was out. He could see faces in a few windows or peering over batwing doors, but most folks had gotten the word by now that hell was about to pop in Santiago. A few dogs milled around in the street, looking for a patch of shade that was scarce this time of the day.

A hot, dry wind had kicked up, lifting dust and shepherding tumbleweeds to and fro, tossing them up onto verandas or lodging them under stock troughs.

The street narrowed as Longarm, Jessie, and Wesley Wade strode into the Mexican side of town. Here were the old, original adobe shacks and mud pens, the cantinas hunched in the brush with well-worn paths between them. There were even fewer people out here than in the Anglo part of Santiago. Longarm saw only one—a young *puta*, maybe twelve years old and wearing a sackcloth dress, barefoot, but with several colorful strings of beads drooping over her small breasts, which were all but revealed by the dress's plunging neckline.

She stood between a cantina's batwing doors, one dusty foot cocked behind the other, her head canted to one side, a bored look on her face. The smell of wood smoke and roasting peppers emanated from the shadows behind her.

The church was on the east end of the town, fronted by a dry fountain with a headless statue of Madre Maria. Longarm shoved Wade into the gap on the church's west side, between the church's crumbling wall and a large, clapboard freight warehouse. Jessie hung back, moving slowly and holding her rifle in both hands, turning to watch the alley mouth behind them.

At the dilapidated church's rear corner, Longarm shoved Wade up against the wall, then, continuing to hold his Winchester snug against the back of the killer's neck, peered around behind the church and into the open area in the chaparral behind it. There was a chicken coop and an old barn back there with a low wall of humped earth around it. Behind the wall stood a half dozen well-armed men in brush jackets, chaps, high-topped boots, and broad-brimmed hats. They were bearded or mustached, and they were all holding rifles.

All except for Buckshot Pete. He was hatless. His

shaggy, salt-and-pepper hair blew around his seasoned forehead. Longarm couldn't see his eyes well from this distance, but he looked grim. Blood dribbled down his left cheek, and his shoulders were stooped. He'd been gone over good.

Longarm felt a keen pain of sorrow for the man. Just when he'd started to get some of his pluck back, they'd taken him down. He was wearing the same ratty garb he'd left the jailhouse in, so he hadn't even had his bath, much less a chance to change his clothes.

Slightly flanking his right side stood Norvell Wade in a crisp suit with a string tie and his white Stetson. He looked nearly as dour as Buckshot Pete, slightly stooped and grim, a bloody white bandage showing on the left side of his neck.

"Where's my son?" the man called above the sawing wind and sifting dust.

Longarm pulled Wesley out away from the church wall, keeping his Winchester snug against the back of the kid's neck. He stayed behind the kid, in case any of the cold steel artists around Wade got the idea they could drill Longarm from that distance of a hundred feet or so. Jessie stood behind Longarm, nearer the church wall and turned sideways so she could watch their backs.

"Send him over here," Norvell Wade called. "When I have my son, I'll send out the sheriff. Don't really know what you want him back for. He's nothin' more than a back-alley lush, but . . ."

Wade grinned tightly, showing his white teeth in his big, red, clean-shaven face.

"And what's your son, Wade?" Fury seared Longarm's ribs to his heart. "What's he but a back-shootin' little privy snipe? It's all he's ever been. All he'll ever be. But since you want him back so bad, you send Buckshot Pete over first."

Norvell Wade stared hard at Longarm. The men on either side of him, including Arroyo Simms, stared, too, canting their heads this way and that, adjusting their grips on their rifles. They squinted against the rising dust, leather dusters and vests flapping with the gusting breeze.

"We send 'em both out at the same time," Wade yelled.

Longarm nodded. The rancher waited until Longarm had slipped his rifle out of the noose behind Wesley's neck then nudged Buckshot Pete ahead with the butt of his rifle. Pete stumbled forward, glanced back at Wade, then continued walking toward the back of the church. Longarm planted the butt of his own rifle against Wesley Wade's back, gave him a shove. The young gunslick stumbled forward, then, getting his feet beneath him, cast a mocking grin back over his left shoulder at Longarm, winking at Jessie.

Jessie told young Wade to do something physically impossible to himself. Wade laughed.

Longarm watched young Wade's back as he strolled across the lot toward his father and the Chain Link shooters. Buckshot Pete walked toward Longarm and Jessie, whose heart Longarm imagined he could hear thudding tensely. Behind Buckshot, Norvell Wade and his men stood holding their rifles, scowling, jaws tense with anticipation.

Frustration pricked along Longarm's spine as Buckshot and young Wade walked toward each other, on a course that would cause them to pass each other about six feet apart and about thirty yards away from Longarm, not directly ahead but a little to the right. As he watched his prisoner drift away toward his father's seasoned shooters, the federal lawman knew that young Wade would be harder than ever to get under lock and key again.

But he wasn't leaving this country without his prisoner.

The thought had no sooner passed through his mind before Buckshot Pete sort of stumbled and lurched forward. The Santiago sheriff jerked to his own left, and then he had his arms around young Wade's waist, bulling him back and sideways. Wesley yelped as he stumbled, throwing his arms out for balance.

Buckshot shouted, "Give 'em hell, Custis!"

As Buckshot and Wade hit the ground at the lip of a dry wash curving between the back of the church and the adobe before which Norvell Wade's men were gathered, Longarm snapped his rifle to his shoulder, instinctively drawing a bead on the deadliest shooter of Wade's bunch, and squeezed the trigger.

The rifle belched. Arroyo Simms had been raising his own rifle. As Longarm's slug punched a nickel-sized hole in the man's forehead, snapping his head back, Arroyo triggered his own rifle into the low adobe wall before him. The slug must have ricocheted off the lip of the wall, because a man to his left gave a yowl and, dropping his carbine, grabbed his elbow.

Jessie gave a shrill, wild yell, dropped to a knee beside Longarm, and began flinging lead toward Wade's crew, her Winchester leaping and smoking in her hands. Longarm racked and fired a second shot as Wade's men ducked down behind the wall, cursing and returning a few wild shots.

As Longarm worked his Winchester, he saw Buckshot Pete and Wesley Wade struggling together at the lip of the dry wash, young Wade heaving himself to his feet and landing a haymaker across Buckshot's left temple. Buckshot spun and dropped, young Wade bellowing madly and clenching his fists.

"Wesley, get over here, ya fool pup!" Norvell Wade shouted from behind the low adobe wall.

Longarm triggered his Winchester. His slug plowed into the wall just right of Wade, and the rancher jerked his head down as bits of adobe sprayed his face. He lifted his head to peer over the wall once more, and his eyes were narrowed with fury, cheeks as red as the bandage over his neck.

As bullets plowed gravel around him and spanged off the church wall flanking him, Longarm ejected the spent cartridge from his rifle's breech. He spared a quick look toward the wash, caught a glimpse of Wesley Wade and Buckshot Pete tumbling over the wash's edge and out of sight.

There was no way that Buckshot was going to take down the young firebrand half his age.

Quickly, Longarm racked a fresh round and continued firing at the adobe wall, over which the half dozen shooters fired their rifles, smoke puffs indicating the location of each. Through his own wafting powder smoke and theirs, Longarm saw blood spurt from a temple, blowing a hat from a head, while another of his triggered rounds punched through a shoulder and sent a shooter bolting straight back away from the wall, dropping his rifle and clutching the bloody hole with his other hand.

As several slugs tore up rocks and gravel in front of Longarm and Jessie, whose own rifle had clicked empty, Longarm yelled, "Get behind the wall, girl. They're gonna blow your fool head off!"

"What about your own?" Jessie shouted as she ran

back behind Longarm, putting the church wall between her and the Wade shooters.

Longarm rammed his right shoulder up against the church wall as two slugs hammered the cracked adobe in front of him, peppering his face with stinging mud slivers.

Thumbing cartridges into her carbine's receiver, Jessie leaned out away from the wall to get a look at Wade's men.

Pulling her head back once more as hot lead stitched the air of the gap between the church and the warehouse, Jessie slapped Longarm's left thigh with the back of her right hand. "You're hit, Custis!"

Longarm looked down.

Blood oozed from a ragged hole in the side of his leg, just above his knee. He'd thought he'd felt a pinch down there but had been too preoccupied with Wade's shooters and Buckshot's dustup with Wesley Wade to give it notice.

Suddenly, he was aware of another burn in his upper right arm. Sure enough, another of Wade's blue whistlers had torn a hole in his shirt about six inches down from his shoulder.

Longarm glanced back at Jessie, who'd dropped to a knee beside him and was canting her head out from the wall as she automatically loaded her carbine.

"How many are still shootin'?" he asked her, ramming his back against the church wall as he reloaded his own repeater.

"Three includin' Wade!"

Longarm thumbed another cartridge through his Winchester's loading gate. Two seasoned shooters and old Wade himself wasn't bad odds. None of those fellas had been all that handy with long guns, anyway—probably being more practiced with six-shooters at close range. Longarm tilted his head out from beside the wall, peering into the wash. He saw nothing but brush, no sign of Buckshot or Wesley Wade.

He didn't have time to dally. Buckshot wouldn't last forever against Wesley, and, losing blood, Longarm himself would soon be too weak to fight.

He slid the last cartridge into his rifle, and levered one up into the chamber. "Cover me!"

"What the hell you think . . . ?"

Jessie let her voice trail off as Longarm stepped out away from the church and took long strides forward, aiming his Winchester straight out from his right shoulder. He walked ten feet, firing three shots quickly as Jessie fired from behind him, her slugs hammering the low adobe wall behind which the shooters were keeping their heads down. When Jessie had emptied her Winchester and he heard her firing pin *ping* on the empty chamber, Longarm dashed forward, holding his Winchester up high across his chest.

He grimaced against the pain in his leg and arm, running hard.

Just as all three of the shooters, including old Wade himself, lifted their heads from behind the wall, Longarm stopped, shot the one farthest left, then, as both Wade and the other killer shouted angrily and brought their own weapons to bear, Longarm bolted forward, running hard once more, and dived over the wall.

Lead screamed around him, one slug kissing the slack of his pants cuff. As he hit the ground behind the wall and rolled, two more slugs blew up dirt around him. He rolled up against the shack and saw both Wade and his sole surviving pistoleer swing their rifles toward him, their faces etched with surprise.

Longarm whipped up the barrel of his Winchester, drew a bead on the center of the blond-bearded pistoleer's chest, and squeezed the trigger. The shooter's Winchester spoke a half second after Longarm's, the shooter's slug hammering the wall just above Longarm's head. The man gritted his teeth, then bellowed, dropping his rifle and clutching the blood-pumping hole in his chest before he flew straight back over the wall, getting hung up by his knees and hanging there so that his legs with their high-topped black boots and silver spurs remained in Longarm's view.

"You sonofabitch!" Norvell Wade bellowed, clicking back the hammer of a long-barreled Army Colt and narrowing one eye as he aimed at Longarm.

Longarm's heart thudded. He cocked his own Winchester, but he knew in the back of his mind that Wade had him dead to rights. As his ejected cartridge arced over his right shoulder and *ping*ed off the shack wall behind him, he looked at Wade, who lifted the corners of his thin mouth in a grim half smile as he steadied his Colt at Longarm's forehead.

The man's own head suddenly exploded, blood and brains flying.

Wade triggered the Colt. The slug hammered the shack wall two feet above Longarm's head, peppering him with mud chips. Wade dropped the gun in the dirt at his feet, and his ruined head sagged, one eye hanging by a thin thread of red viscera. He fell to his knees, chin brushing his chest, then fell straight down in the dirt.

Longarm bit back a curse at the pain in his arm and leg, and pushed himself to his feet. He looked over the wall to see Jessie standing about ten feet away, holding her smoking Winchester straight out from her right shoulder. She was hatless, and her tawny hair blew around in the dusty wind.

Slowly, she lowered her rifle.

Longarm heaved a relieved sigh and looked around at the six Chain Link men lying in dirty, bloody piles around him.

"Pa!" Jessie said, lowering her Winchester and running toward the dry wash.

She stopped suddenly. Buckshot Pete climbed up out of the wash, grunting and snarling like an old bobcat, pulling himself up by greasewood branches. Over his right shoulder he carried Wesley Wade. When he gained the top of the wash, he stepped forward, staggering under the weight, and flung Wade off his shoulder. The young firebrand piled up in the dirt like a hundred-pound sack of potatoes.

Breathing hard, Buckshot looked from his daughter to Longarm. His face was bloody and bruised, both lips and one eye swollen.

"Don't worry, I didn't cheat the hangman," Buckshot said, leaning forward, hands on his knees. "He's just catchin' thirty winks."

"Buckshot, you crazy sonofabitch." Longarm leaned back against the shack wall for support.

Jessie ran to her father and hugged him. Buckshot grinned and wrapped his arms around the girl's waist, holding her tight.

"*Custiiiis!*"

Longarm turned to see Raquella sprinting toward him from the gap between the church and the warehouse. She came running across the open ground, her dark eyes worried, ample breasts bouncing around inside her low-cut dress like two piglets in a gunnysack.

"I heard the shooting."

She climbed over the wall, bending down so that her dress billowed out from her chest, giving his pain-racked eyes a soothing snootful. She hurried over to him, her eyes raking him, catching on the wounds.

"You're bleeding!"

"Just flesh wounds, Raquella."

She draped his left arm around her neck. "I will help you to the doctor."

"Hold on," Jessie growled, stepping over the uncon-scious Wesley Wade and striding over from where she'd left her father. "I'll get him over to the sawbones, Mrs. Mayfair. Why don't you go on back over to the hotel and tend your husband or boil some sheets or somesuch?"

The two women parried glares.

"Hold on," Longarm said as Raquella helped him over the low wall. "You can both get me over to the sawbones."

As Jessie ducked under one of his brawny arms, and Raquella straightened under the other, he leaned into both girls and glanced over his shoulder at Buckshot Pete. "Can you manage with Wesley by your lonesome, Pete?"

The sheriff of Santiago chuckled as he watched Long-arm being hauled off by the women. "What the hell choice do I have?"